A WHITE CHRISTMAS

ELITE MEN OF MANHATTAN CHRISTMAS NOVELLA

MISSY WALKER

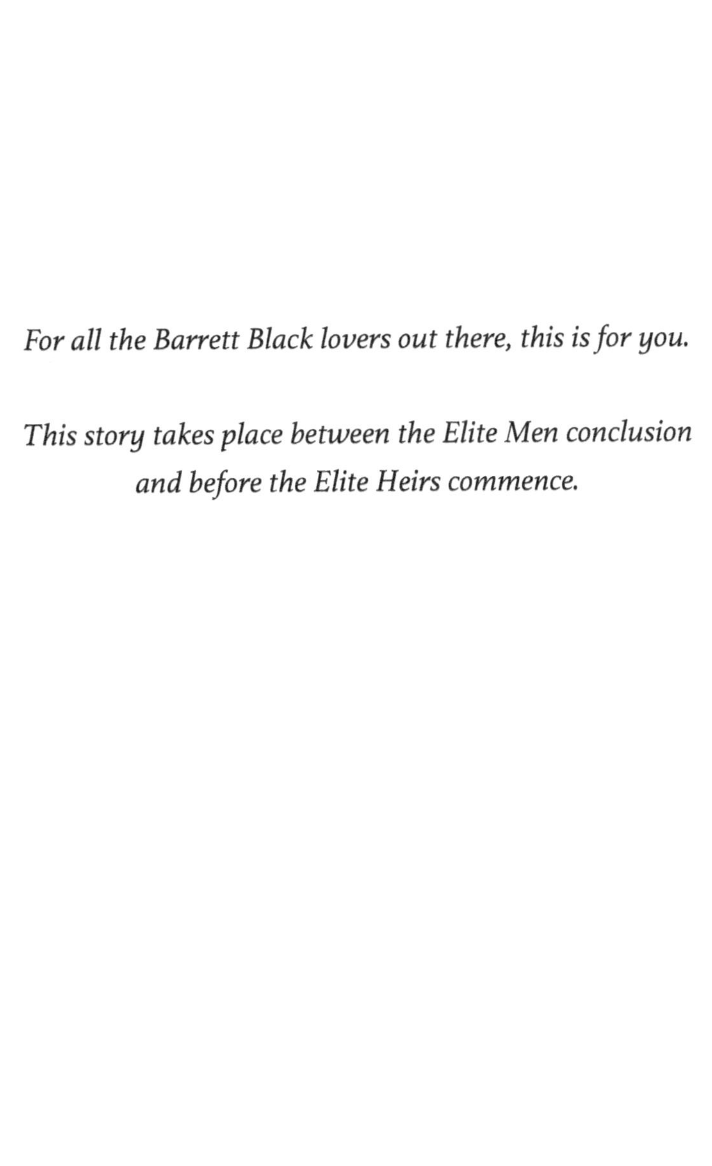

For all the Barrett Black lovers out there, this is for you.

This story takes place between the Elite Men conclusion and before the Elite Heirs commence.

1

———

LOURDE

There was nothing like stepping into the Vail cabin for the first time on each visit. I had lost track of the number of vacations and holidays we'd spent there. Every arrival felt like the first one. I was full of excitement and anticipation, looking forward to the good times we were going to have.

Especially now, with Christmas only five days away. It had taken a lot of schedule juggling to coordinate, and some of us would still have to work a little while we were here, but for the most part, the entire family and friends had managed to clear the entire span from now until New Year's Day.

I was first inside, looking around to check out the results of the decorating I had worked out with the cabin's staff. Just as I requested, the twenty-foot tree sat in the front window so wide it almost blocked the entire view. It would glow spectacularly at night and would make an absolutely stunning effect while set against snowcapped peaks and towering pines.

Out of just about everything, this was what I'd worried about the most. It wasn't easy, leaving something this critical in the hands of people thousands of miles away, even though we'd worked with the same staff ever since Barrett first bought the cabin a few years after Colton was born. *I want to make family memories,* he had told me at the time, and I agreed.

What I didn't realize then was that he'd bought a cabin that was more like a castle. Two enormous wings jutted off from the central hub where the living room, dining room, and kitchen sat. There were ten bedrooms, five in each wing, meaning it was the perfect place for large gatherings like the one we would enjoy this year.

"It looks great in here." Barrett followed two staff members inside, directing them to leave the luggage in our respective rooms. "Now, aren't you glad you spent all that time choosing the right tree? It's gorgeous. And these garlands," he added, admiring the fresh pine boughs hung in the doorways and decorating the railing leading upstairs.

"I do sort of wish we had been able to decorate it ourselves, but…" I craned my neck to look up at the top of the tree, where an angel dressed in silver was perched, "… I think we'd end up getting nosebleeds if we tried to climb that high."

His arms wrapped around me from behind, and his lips found my neck. "We could always get a smaller tree to put elsewhere if that's what you want. I'm sure I could arrange to have lights and ornaments delivered. Whatever makes you happy."

It was a nice idea, but it left me feeling a little crestfallen. "No," I decided, my attention falling on Colton and Sienna as they slowly made their way from the SUV and up the front steps. It didn't help that they both had their noses buried in their phones. Half the fun of decorating the tree was doing it together as a family. Something told me they'd be less than eager.

"I'm telling you," I muttered, shaking my head as we watched them approach. "They'll both end up in one of those CCTV videos where you see someone walking straight into a mall fountain because their nose was in their phone."

We shared a quiet laugh as he turned me in his

arms. "This is going to be an ideal holiday, Dollface," he predicted. "Even if they're both growing up too fast."

We had been together for almost twenty years, which meant I shouldn't have been surprised he was able to read my thoughts. "I can't help it," I admitted in a whisper. "It's not easy, knowing things aren't the same and never will be. Nobody told me the last Christmas they were both innocent little kids would be the last Christmas. Do you know what I mean?"

"There's no warning," he agreed, wearing a sad smile. "So there's another new normal to adjust to. We'll get through it. We always do."

The years had not done anything to change the way my heart swelled at the look he got in his eye. A wicked little grin tugged the corners of his mouth as he lowered his head to my ear. "And there are things to be said for having more time to ourselves, Mrs. Black. It's been a long time since we christened every room in the penthouse."

He made a good point, and I dissolved into giggles when his mouth roamed my neck. "This mountain air always brings out the animal in you." I laughed while he made animal noises like he was devouring me.

"Come on," Colton grumbled as he entered the cabin. "Nobody wants to see that."

Typical teenager. "Would you rather have parents who never speak to each other?" Barrett asked a little more sharply than necessary. I normally defended our son from the stern things he said. I always thought he was a little too hard on Colton, but then I was a mother. I was supposed to be the peacemaker.

"What's taking your sister so long?" I asked, looking out the window again. Sienna was typing furiously on her phone, her chestnut brown locks covering the sides of her face. Something was off with her, not that she would ever tell me what. At fifteen, I might as well have been her mortal enemy. When I looked at her, instead of seeing the leggy, pretty teenager I had raised so far, I saw the happy little girl who loved making Christmas cookies and wore her pajamas inside out the night before a projected snowstorm, hoping that would make the snow fall harder.

"She's waiting for Rose." Colton, meanwhile, started up the steps with a bag slung over his shoulder. "Usual bedrooms?" he called out.

"Yes, you're sharing your usual room with Evan." Evan had ridden with us from the jet and now brought up the rear, carrying a pair of suitcases up from the SUV. He was a nice kid, always polite and helpful.

"What a shame our son doesn't take after him," Barrett murmured with a sigh.

"Evan is a good influence, but you can only lead a horse to water," I reminded him.

The rest of the group arrived moments later, with a trio of SUVs pulling up in the circular front courtyard. Outside, the trees were also decorated, strung with lights that would go on at dusk. I could hardly wait to see them twinkle.

I heard Pepper as soon as she stepped out of the car, tossing her curls over her shoulder in the middle of delivering a fiery speech. What was she so worked up about? I had no idea. I only knew her son, Lucian, looked a little downcast as he followed his mother out of the SUV.

When Evan opened the front door, I heard Pepper's voice floating up. "What Colton and Noah and Evan do is their business," she insisted, wagging a finger in Lucian's face. "They are older than you. Hanging out with them during the day is fine, but if they want to go out at night, you are staying in. No excuses."

It was clear Connor wouldn't be any help since

all he did was shrug when Lucian gave him a pleading look. "Poor kid," I whispered, watching his face fall. "Maybe we can convince Colton—"

"You go right ahead if you think you can convince Colton of anything," Barrett interrupted as he removed his coat. "He's going to do whatever he wants no matter what we tell him. If Connor and Pepper want Lucian to stay behind because they know Colton will only get him into trouble, that's their business. I can't blame them."

Since pushing the issue would only end up in an argument, I let it go, choosing instead to greet Sienna when she walked in. "There you are. When would you like to go shopping?" I asked. "Didn't you say on the jet you wanted to pick up a couple of extra gifts?"

The girl looked at me like I was a slug. "Why are you eavesdropping on my conversations?" she asked.

"You think you and your cousins are quiet when you get together?" Barrett countered, rolling his eyes at me. "I don't think earplugs would help drown you girls out."

"We're just going to go together." Sienna wrapped her arms around herself, shoulders hunched. "It's not like it's a big deal."

"Well, your aunts and I were planning on going

out too. I don't see any reason why we couldn't all shop together." I forced myself to pretend her disdain didn't sting a little as my brother led the way into the cabin with Pepper and Lucian behind him.

Pepper let out a dramatic gasp once she noticed the tree. "God, Lourde, it's exquisite!" She took a deep breath, letting out a happy sigh. "There is nothing like the smell of a fresh tree."

Connor, meanwhile, laughed as our eyes met across the room. "Are you thinking about what I'm thinking about?" he asked.

I burst out laughing. "Don't worry. I asked them to check carefully for any nests that might be inside." When Pepper raised an eyebrow, I explained, "One Christmas, we were treated to a little family of squirrels that happened to be living in our tree."

"They waited until Christmas morning to pop out and say hi." Connor was still laughing as he wrapped an arm around Pepper's waist. "I can't believe I never told you about that."

"You probably didn't tell her because it would mean describing you running through the house, screaming like somebody had set you on fire," I pointed out, laughing harder when he scowled. "How old were you? Thirteen? Fourteen?" From the corner of my eye, I noticed the way Lucian grinned before heading upstairs with Evan. I couldn't help the kid deal with being younger than everybody else, but at least I could give him something to smile about.

Ari and Olivia followed with Rose and Noah, who hadn't stopped bickering since they got on the jet. Olivia noticed but only shook her head. Some fights weren't worth waging, and the rivalry between brothers and sisters qualified. They were still muttering back and forth on their way up to their rooms.

Meanwhile, Ari was on the phone, taking a work call from the way his mouth twisted in a scowl. He hung back outside while the rest of his family came in.

"I can't give him any shit about it," Olivia admitted when she noticed us watching him. "I mean, I don't want him throwing it back in my face when I tell him we're going over to the hotel later. I'm going upstairs to freshen up."

The hotel. Just thinking about it made my palms sweat. The Schwartz family were acquaintances of ours. Their daughter, Penelope, attended the same prep school as the rest of the kids, and we had run into them at multiple events over the years. When

Alex mentioned the hotel he'd bought here in Vail, describing the work that would need to be done to update it after he made the purchase, Barrett hadn't hesitated to throw his hat in the ring. Alex made it easy, gladly accepting the offer when Barrett pledged to have the sprawling hotel brought up-to-date and code by the end of January. The changes would actually be completed ahead of schedule.

All that was left now was to redecorate it for the first time since before Barrett and I started sneaking around behind everyone's backs. A lot had changed since then, including the fact that Olivia and I were now in a prime position to transform the place and get our interior decorating business in front of countless more eyes. It was the sort of job that could end up in magazines and effectively double or triple our potential client base.

We had never taken on anything this enormous, but I knew we could handle it. The tricky part would be convincing Alex Schwartz that we could. I was feeling hopeful, though, since he and Barrett had a nice working relationship. It could only help.

Evelyn and Magnus joined us, with Aria and Valentina gushing over what they planned to wear to the black-tie New Year's Eve gala we were attending. "It's got a slit up to here," Valentina explained, touching her fingertips to the place on her thigh where the slit would begin.

"Excuse me?" Magnus bellowed. Valentina must have assumed he was farther behind her rather than directly on her heels. "Exactly what do you plan on wearing in public?"

"It's a nice dress, Dad." Valentina shot a worried glance toward her twin. The two of them always had each other's backs. "It's classy."

"It's really nice, Dad," Aria agreed. "Even I don't think it's too much."

Evelyn chuckled softly, placing a hand on her husband's shoulder. Funny, the way he visibly relaxed at her touch. "Let them be young," she urged with a playful laugh. "I wish I'd had that kind of confidence when I was their age." She winked at the girls, telling me the argument was effectively over. They wasted no time scrambling upstairs, whispering to each other.

Magnus rubbed his temples, then slid out of his coat. "How many times do we have to have this talk? We are a united front, right?"

"When it comes to the major things, yes," she agreed. "But honey, I would challenge you right now to find a black-tie-worthy dress without either a low-cut neckline or a thigh-high slit. At least she won't be running around with her boobs hanging out."

He winced hard enough that I had to cover my mouth to hide a laugh. "She has a point," I teased, sharing a secret smile with my sister-in-law. She was a pro at getting around his prickly nature, though those of us who knew him best understood the prickles only existed on the surface, much like the rest of our hunkholes. At the end of the day, his wife and girls were his world.

"Clearly, I'm outnumbered," he grumbled, glancing toward the stairs. "The usual room assignments?"

"You've got it," I told him. Evelyn took his hand and walked with him up the staircase. Her laughter told me she was still teasing him.

Barrett was chuckling as he checked out the fully stocked wine and liquor cabinet. "It's a good thing we made sure this was ready for us," he mused with a smirk once the living room quieted down. "Something tells me we are all going to want a drink or two this week."

2

———

BARRETT

"Are you sure you want to come in with us?" Was I not supposed to notice the look exchanged between my wife and her business partner as we approached the Schwartz property, currently in its final stages of renovations? They were treating me like the third wheel, the out-of-touch helicopter parent they wished they could ditch. At least, that was the impression I got from Olivia as she flipped her blonde hair over her shoulder in the back seat, sitting next to Lourde.

Lourde cleared her throat. "I don't want to make it look like we expect favoritism," she fretted. "It might look suspicious if we visit along with you."

I swiveled in the front passenger seat, looking back at her. "I already had my visit scheduled for this morning before we arrived. It has nothing to do with you ladies."

"Has he said anything about us?" Olivia asked. Lourde rolled her eyes as I turned to face the front, telling me she didn't approve of the question. She had probably already warned Olivia against asking it, but Olivia tended to do her own thing when she felt like it.

"We have not talked about the decorating," I explained. "That's not my area."

"So, no word of confidence?"

"Lay off him." Lourde sighed. "The next thing you know, you'll be asking whether Alex likes us or like-likes us. You sound like you're in middle school, crushing on some boy."

Olivia snickered. "I wish it was that low stakes." From the corner of my eye, I watched her check her appearance in a handheld mirror. "I can't wait to get to the spa. I hope they're ready to pull out all the stops."

I left them to their conversation, which soon rounded the corner, and switched topics to salon appointments and whatever else they were concerned about in preparation for the New Year's Eve party.

The Schwartz project represented a milestone

for my company, which I hoped to parlay into a solid revenue stream. New construction was one thing, but it was also extremely pricey, not to mention time-consuming. We had identified an untapped market in hotel and resort owners purchasing defunct or outdated properties. They could update and renovate for a lot less than starting from scratch, which could only be a good thing when it came to snapping up new customers. It wasn't possible to book rooms in a hotel that hadn't opened yet.

My team was off through the rest of the year, with plans to return the first week in January. After that, it would be another two weeks or so, barring any weather emergencies. At that point, the whirlwind of decorating would begin. I'd kept the questions I had about what was taking so long to decide who Alex would trust to launch his new property into a new era to myself, but they percolated in the back of my mind by the time we reached the turn-in leading up to the hotel.

"Oh, Barrett." Olivia touched a hand to her chest while her mouth fell open. "It is stunning!"

I had to agree. We had taken an old, Tudor-style structure and turned it into a Swiss chalet. "If you think that's impressive," I told her. "You should see what we did inside. I swear, some of that plumbing might as well have been from the nineteenth centu-ry." We had also demolished and rebuilt several small cabins on the property, along with constructing a recreation room, a library, and a small movie theater so guests wouldn't have to leave the property during a heavy storm if they were looking for ways to pass the time.

Lourde made a noise that brought to mind one word. *Hunger.* "You have no idea how much I want to get my hands on this." The hands she talked about were now clasped in her lap, encased in leather gloves. The leather squeaked when she clinched him tighter. "The things we could do here."

"Well, from what I understand, Alex has a fairly unlimited budget, and that is all I'm going to say," I added when their eyes lit up in unison. They might as well have been sharpening their knives and tucking in their bibs, ready to feast.

I couldn't lie to myself that it didn't turn me on a little watching my wife kick ass and feel so passionate about her work. Of all the many things she had shown me over the course of our marriage, one of the most surprising lessons was how sexy it was to observe her when she was deep in the flow of a new project. Overhearing her phone calls with vendors when she wouldn't back down for something she wanted and the high standards she and Olivia had set. More than one of those phone calls had been followed up by me practically mauling her in her office. I couldn't resist.

"He's supposed to be here, waiting," I murmured, noticing his car, along with a handful of others, parked near the main entrance.

"Is he supposed to be talking to potential contractors today?" Lourde asked, craning her neck to see through the window. "There I was, thinking we were getting a leg up by showing our faces."

"I really don't know. I wouldn't worry about it, though," I added, reaching back and squeezing her knee when she wouldn't look my way. "He would be a complete fucking idiot if he didn't hire you for the job."

"You're right." She set up straighter, pushing strands of brown hair away from her shoulders as we stopped. I climbed out first, opened the rear door, and extended a hand to her, then to Olivia.

"There he is. My miracle worker." Alex strode out to greet us, wearing a broad grin that preceded his warm handshake. "Glad to see you getting away for a little while. If anyone deserves it, it's you."

"Is there such a thing as a relaxing vacation when a guy brings his teenagers along with him?" I countered, and we shared a laugh. His daughter, Penelope, was around the same age as Colton. We had commiserated more than once over the challenges of raising decent, responsible kids in this world.

"I have the family up here through the new year, as well," he explained. "I didn't want to be too far from my new baby." With that, he turned toward the front of the building, releasing a satisfied sigh. "It's gorgeous. Beyond my wildest dreams."

"I hope you don't mind," Lourde offered as she stepped up beside me. "I've heard so much about the work going on out here. I had to see it for myself."

"Oh, of course. It's good to see you." He shook her hand, then Olivia's, with the three of them chatting amiably about next semester and whether the kids had chosen their colleges yet.

"You think we could take a peek inside?" Olivia asked, biting her lip against a brilliant smile. "I promise we won't touch anything. But you have to know we are salivating over the possibility of working with you."

"No pressure," Lourde added. I could tell she was a little squeamish over Olivia's frank announcement, but I would've done the same thing if that were me. Why bother beating around the bush?

They wanted this project. Why not be honest about it?

"Oh, not to worry. I don't feel pressured. By all means, go in and look around." We followed them inside, where the stunned gasps I'd been expecting were right on cue.

The entire lobby had been rebuilt, featuring a stunning peaked roof that stretched three stories above the lobby. The front wall was composed entirely of windows that allowed brilliant sunshine to stream inside, making the salvaged pine floors gleam.

Lourde's eyes sparkled in that light as she turned in a slow circle. "This is stunning. Really breathtaking. And this view!" She stepped up close to the window, admiring the snow-frosted town below us.

"We're pretty happy with it," Alex confirmed.

The girls wandered off, chatting with their heads close together. A couple of employees sat at the front desk, going over things, and I paid no attention until one of them stood up and gave me the chance to get a good look at him for the first time. *Kelvin fucking Barnes.*

Incredible, really, how suddenly my mood could change. *This piece of shit.* Of all times for him to skulk around, but then he didn't like to miss an opportunity to shove himself in his brother-in-law's face, like the pissant kid in school who couldn't stop sucking up to the teacher.

He watched Olivia and Lourde progress down the hall into the east wing. Anything Alex had to say fell on deaf ears as I watched every move Kelvin made. Every twitch on his face, which right then I would've loved to cave in. Clearly, he hadn't noticed me, or he wouldn't outright ogle my wife's ass.

Or would he? Because he didn't look very surprised when he slowly turned our way to discover Alex and me standing at the opposite end of the cathedral-size space. "Oh. Barrett. To what do we owe the pleasure?" he asked, rounding the desk, heading our way wearing an easy grin that did nothing to disguise what a weaselly piece of shit he was.

He was still pissed over the fact that his brother-in-law chose me instead of him to handle this renovation. I would have felt bad for the guy if he wasn't such an asshole, resentful of a so-called outsider coming in and doing the work when technically Alex was an outsider too. This was his first property in Colorado, with the rest of them out in the New York Catskills.

All of that and more passed over his face as he

extended a hand. "And there I was, disappointed that you wouldn't grace these halls again now that the refurbishment is complete," he concluded. I had never met a man who was so due for a punch.

"Almost complete," I reminded him. "Anyway, I'm in town with the family over the holidays and thought I would stop in. What brings you here?" I asked since I knew damn well he didn't have a job with his brother-in-law's company.

Alex jumped in. "Kelvin is helping me manage the transition once we get rolling on decorating and the press outreach." The girl still sitting behind the desk called out to him, and he shrugged. "No rest for the wicked."

"Don't let me hold you up," I told him. "I only wanted to make sure you were happy with everything around here."

"Happy? I'm overjoyed!" He sounded that way, too, and his laughter echoed around the space as he walked away.

Kelvin turned toward me again, his brows lifting. From the golden hair to the deep, wind-burned suntan that made his gray eyes leap out, he could've posed for a spread in an ad for ski equipment. "I understand your wife and her business partner are in the running for the decorating contract."

He would love nothing more than to get a rise out of me. The man didn't bother pretending to be anything other than who he was. I gritted my teeth and replied, "That's my wife's business. I have nothing to do with it."

"Oh, sure. You stopped by to say hello and happened to bring the two of them with you. Completely innocent." He snickered as he looked down the hall again while I considered breaking his jaw. "Well, I can say this much. It will be nice to see her around the place if she gets the job. She brightens it up."

"And now that you've managed to work your way into your brother-in-law's new property, you're in a perfect position to see her, aren't you?" I nodded slowly, offering soft applause. "Isn't it nice, falling back on family ties to make ends meet when there's a slump in business?"

His expression hardened the way I'd intended. "You know what? I'll do you a favor. I'll recommend her for the job. Just to show you there are no hard feelings. Clearly, Alex hired the best company for the renovations."

As if I'd ever believe he meant that. "I'm sure she doesn't need your help."

"Oh, it's the least I can do." Looking over his

shoulder to where Lourde and Olivia were deep in conversation, he added, "Like I said. She'll brighten up the place a little." Then, turning back to me, he continued, "With her decorating skills, of course."

Alex saved his life by calling him over, leaving me to stare holes into the back of his head as he sauntered away. If Lourde got the job, it would mean knowing this piece of shit was going out of his way to be in front of her. It wasn't as if this had never happened. I was married to a beautiful woman whose stunning looks had only improved over time.

But this? This was on a different level. I couldn't tell her not to take the job, but I couldn't stomach the thought of her being here with him, either.

Not for a minute.

"Where are you tonight?" Lourde waved a playful hand in front of my face, giggling when I stirred myself out of my stupor. "I swear, you haven't listened to a single thing anyone has said tonight."

I looked around the long dining table. "It doesn't seem like anyone else has noticed," I pointed out since the conversation was as lively as it had been all night.

The boys compared notes, talking about their plans on the ski slopes. The girls liked skiing, too, but at the moment, they were more concerned with buying last-minute presents during a shopping trip to town. Once or twice, I noticed Sienna gazing off, distracted, and I had to wonder what she was feeling so depressed about. Lourde had tried to get through to her with no success. There was even less of a chance of her wanting to talk to her father about whatever it was.

"You know what I think?" Connor grinned down the table, looking at me. "I think we need to take these kids out on the slopes and show them what real skiing is about. Not this bunny slope bullshit," he announced.

"Come on, Dad," Lucian groaned. "None of us have been on the bunny slopes in years." He had a way of taking it personally whenever someone talked about age since all he wanted was to be considered one of the guys. To be taken seriously.

Pepper swatted at her husband with her napkin and shook her head. "So help me, Connor Diamond. If my son breaks his neck out there because you challenged him to a triple black diamond run or some stupid shit, I will cut off your balls and wear them as a pendant around my neck."

"Quick," Ari joked. "Check under the table, see if he's cupping himself for protection." Even Connor had to laugh at that, along with the rest of us.

"I promise," he crooned, wrapping his arms around his wife as she scowled. "I'll make sure he's in one piece heading into the new year."

"I love it when they talk about me like I'm not here," Lucian muttered to Rose, who giggled.

I wished I could feel like I was a part of things, but that run-in with Kelvin earlier today was like an ulcer growing in me. Lourde wanted this job so much she could taste it. I was proud of her. I wanted her to succeed. But at what cost? If I mentioned my misgivings about Kelvin, she would laugh it off and remind me she could handle herself. *I didn't grow up surrounded by creeps in New York and not learn how to take care of myself.* Like it was that easy—this wasn't a matter of flipping off a catcaller in the middle of the sidewalk.

"Come on." She clapped her hands briskly, then stood. "Since the staff worked so hard to put this amazing feast together for us tonight, the least we can do is clean up after ourselves. That means *you*," she added when Colton snickered.

"Me?" he asked, looking around. "I thought that was the point of having a staff."

I hadn't cared much either way until he broke out that bullshit excuse. "The fact that you would say something like that in front of all these people is exactly why you need to get up right now and start getting plates together."

Evelyn offered a tiny smile from halfway down the table, and I got the feeling we were thinking along the same lines. We hadn't grown up the way our children were growing up. There were no house-keepers and no trips to Vail for Christmas. It was a fine line we both treaded, wanting our kids to grow up with decent values and work ethics but knowing how seductive it was to sit back in luxury. It was all they had ever known.

Sienna jumped to her feet and nudged Colton as she walked past him. "Stop being a baby."

"Why do you have to name call?" he retorted, grumbling as he began to gather plates. It was clear from the way he glared at me every now and then he resented every second of it, but he knew his sister had a point. He was acting like a child and in front of his friend, Evan.

"Don't be so hard on him," Lourde whispered once he was in the kitchen, and all I could do was snort. If she had her way, he would never be held accountable for any of the dumb shit he did. For the sake of keeping the peace, I nodded in agreement, though it did nothing to change the irritation I was struggling with.

Who was I most irritated with? That was the problem. Colton's behavior would have set my teeth on edge at any other time, but I probably wouldn't have bothered commenting if it wasn't for what I was already battling in my head. Bringing it up with Lourde when we were alone was all I could do. Otherwise, I would spend this entire trip on edge, ready to hit something or someone.

Until then, there was no choice but to spend the rest of the night feeling separated from everyone else, lost in thought.

3

LOURDE

"It's a shame that women hit their sexual peak so much later in life than men do." Barrett's hands worked the slippery camisole up to my chest, raising my arms so he could take it off. He wasted no time cupping my breasts, massaging, tweaking the nipples until I sucked in a sharp breath.

"I might not have been at my peak... but I didn't hear you complaining when we first started doing this." Bracing my palms against his chest, I settled into a rhythm and angle that always did the trick. It never failed to make electricity hum through me as his thick head rubbed my G-spot while I ground against his base. I moved slowly, taking my time to build myself up, knowing it would be so much more explosive that way.

"So fucking hot," he whispered, staring up at me. It was one thing to feel him moving inside me, but when our eyes met, and that connection was established, there was a pleasure so much deeper than the physical. The kind that reached way into my soul and reminded me this was what we were all about.

We had always connected on a deeper level, even back before we had the first clue about life. We only thought we did back then, the way young people did. There was still a lifetime's worth of living, loving, compromising, and working together ahead of us.

Getting through all of it and still being able to come together like this... at the end of the day, that was what it was all about. Or at the beginning of the day, since Barrett had woken me up the way he'd been waking me up for years. The man had turned me into Pavlov's dog, salivating at the pressure of his erection against my ass while he caressed every inch of me.

"That's right, nice and slow," he urged, looking down between us to watch himself disappear inside me. He slid a thumb between us, and a moment later, the welcome pressure against my clit and the tingling sensation that built had my head falling back.

"Yes," I gasped out on a heavy breath, rocking harder, more determined.

"Make yourself come on my cock," he growled out, teasing my clit. I covered his hand massaging my breast, squeezing, silently telling him what I needed. It wasn't enough. I needed more, rocking faster and slamming down harder. The tension in my core built until I had to bite down on my lip to quiet the cries rising in my throat.

His hips jerked upward to match my strokes, and it all exploded. Sweetness flooded my body and made it sing with every shockwave that rolled through me. "Yes... God, yes..." I whimpered while Barrett lost control and gave himself over to his release.

"Coming... fuck!" He took hold of me and pulled me down until I was stretched out on top of him, his arms clutching me tight against his chest as the first rush of warmth filled me. His heart pounded the way mine did, erratic and leaving us breathless.

I was still lying across his chest when he took a deep breath that made me rise and fall. "As far as I'm concerned, I've crossed everything off my to-do list. I might not get out of bed."

Opening my eyes, I gazed out the bedroom window at what was becoming a brilliant, beautiful morning. It didn't take much to imagine spending the day like this, watching the shadows change as the sun traveled through the sky. "Let's make it a point to do that at least once before New Year's. For now, I'm going shopping with the girls."

"I guess I'll have to find something to do without you, Dollface." His lips brushed the top of my head, and I smiled, closing my eyes again and soaking in the moment.

"There will be skaters at the ice rink tonight," I murmured. "Maybe we can go down and watch together."

"Sure. Will you get any skiing in this week? How about tomorrow?" he asked as he stroked my back. He needed to stop doing that, or else I was going to fall asleep.

"We'll see. I want to wrap your gifts, and having you out of the cabin will make that easier." I folded my arms across his chest and grinned down at him. "Have you been naughty or nice this year?"

Brushing strands of hair away from my face, he winked. "You know the answer to that one. This year, last year. Probably next year too."

"WHAT ARE YOU SAYING?" I looked at the rest of the group, then back at my daughter. Had she lapsed into a different language? Because I could not genuinely process what I heard come from her mouth.

"It's not that big of a deal." Sienna rolled her eyes to the ceiling. "We just want to sit at a table not attached to you guys. The parents, the daughters."

Why? I had enough pride not to ask. They wanted to be adults, and there were enough people their age hanging out together in the village without their parents to make them self-conscious. I had noticed it while we were shopping, the way the girls ditched us as soon as possible whenever we entered a store, then walked yards behind us on the sidewalks.

What did I expect? A warm, family event? Some lovely Christmas scene? Certainly, the village itself was beyond lovely, like the sort of snowy, twinkling dream that holiday romance movies were based on. For all I knew, this was where the writers got their inspiration.

Sienna sighed, a little impatient. "We're just going to sit at the table next to you guys instead of pushing them together. Why are you making it into something?"

"Of course, go right ahead," I relented. She was right. It would only matter if I made a big deal about it.

We were soon led through a busy, beautifully decorated dining room. Twinkling trees added to the festive air, and the tinsel strong on the branches swayed gently every time someone passed. I vaguely recognized a few faces, people we were acquainted with socially who also came out for the holidays.

"Oh my God," Rose whispered somewhere behind me. "Penny Schwartz is here with her mom."

Immediately, my attention was piqued at the mention of the name. A glance at Olivia told me she heard, too, and her eyes darted around the room until she found the people in question sitting at a table near the window.

It wasn't only Penelope and Grace Schwartz sitting there. Grace's brother, Kelvin, was having lunch with them. His golden hair glowed like a beacon, and his rich laughter drowned out the chatter elsewhere. A sense of discomfort tried to take hold, but I shook it off. Some people had an uncomfortable aura, and he was one of them.

"Here we are, ladies." Our perky server stopped

near a pair of tables with enough room between them for someone to walk through. It wasn't like we would be sitting on the opposite end of the room from our daughters. That didn't do anything to help me shake the sense of being unneeded as we settled in.

"Let it go," Evelyn whispered as we sat down at the square table. "It's not worth it. This is something they all go through." Was I that obvious?

"We always wanted independence when we were teenagers, don't forget," Pepper pointed out. "Considering some of the things they could be up to, this is nothing."

She made a good point. There were always whispers running through our social world, like thin streams of running water underground. Invisible, but very much there, always present. Kids who took a semester off of school in order to attend rehab. That was a big one. Secret pregnancies, DUIs—long 'vacations' meant to cover up getting out of town after bad behavior. As much as it worried me, knowing how wild Colton could be, he wouldn't be stupid enough to get caught up in anything like that.

Or was that what I needed to tell myself? There were times I just wasn't sure.

"Did you notice him yesterday?" Olivia was still

focused on Kelvin, looking his way from behind her menu. If I didn't know any better, I would think she was checking him out, staring at him like she was.

"It was kind of hard not to," I whispered, looking over but trying to play it off. "He was staring pretty openly. I could feel his eyes on the back of my head."

"Who is he?" Evelyn asked.

"Alex Schwartz's brother-in-law," I explained, looking down at my menu when Penelope glanced our way.

Evelyn snorted. "Oh, the one who thought he had that reconstruction job in the bag. Magnus was talking about him."

"Exactly. He gives me the creeps," I admitted, even shivering a little when I thought about it. What was worse, something I didn't want to talk about with the girls sitting so close to us, was how Barrett glared at him. Did he honestly think I would give this man a second glance? If I didn't already know how protective and possessive my husband could be, I might actually feel a little insulted.

"Okay, let's not talk about creeps and weirdos anymore." Pepper ordered a bottle of wine from a passing server, and I was glad to let her change the subject.

The four of us went through the list of what we

still wanted to pick up today, sharing a bottle of Chablis while we did. "The watch I bought for Barrett should be engraved by Christmas Eve," I mused, making a note on my phone. "And I can pick up the you-know-what for you-know-who at the same time."

I glanced toward my daughter, who made it clear there was no reason for me to be discreet. Her nose was buried in her phone. I wanted to buy a pair of sapphire earrings I'd seen in the jewelry store since they looked a lot like a favorite pair of mine. At the moment, I wondered if she would ever wear them.

"I'm not sure why I bother," I admitted, my heart sinking as I reached for my glass of wine. "She truly couldn't care less right now. The worst part is, I'm not sure she would be honest with me if I asked what's going on."

"You know how it is when they're that age. Everything is the end of the world," Olivia pointed out, finally peeling her attention away from Kelvin. "When I think back on what was important to me at that age, I have to cringe."

"Do you think maybe we'll feel that way when we're even older?" I asked. "Will we look back and wonder why we ever cared so much about decorating Alex Schwartz's new hotel?"

Her eyes narrowed while her mouth twitched in a smirk she couldn't suppress. "Don't even joke like that. Being embarrassed over a teenage crush is one thing, but business is business."

The more I thought about it, the more I needed this new job. While our business was healthy and bustling, we had fallen into a rut. We needed something to shake us up, to get us out of our old patterns and habits. Of course, the fact that we'd been in business all these years and been so successful was nothing to complain about, but even the most delicious chocolate cake would get boring day after day. Variety was the spice of life. Besides, I had too much time to brood when there wasn't something actively challenging me, and work simply hadn't challenged me that way in ages.

When it came time to order, the girls went first, and I tried not to pay attention when Sienna ordered, but it was impossible not to. "You're not hungry?" I asked in a low voice once the server turned her attention to the twins. "Are you only getting a side salad?"

"What about it? God. I can't even eat what I want to eat?" Rolling her eyes, she went back to her phone, shooting Rose a meaningful look. They were texting back and forth about us while sitting at the next table over. I had half a mind to threaten going back to the cabin, but that sort of tactic wouldn't work anymore. She was too old for it.

"Let it go," Evelyn muttered under her breath. "The harder you push, the harder she'll push back. Ask me how I know."

I couldn't help but reach out and grasp the thin shred of hope she was dangling. "This is how it was for you with the twins a couple of years ago?" How had she survived it?

Her soft, familiar laughter rang out. "Are you kidding me? I've had so many doors slammed in my face over the past several years, I'm practically immune to it at this point."

"Same here," Olivia agreed. "Though I only have one daughter slamming them. No offense, but I'm sort of glad for that."

"Since we're all making confessions," Pepper quipped. "Let me just say I'm glad I only have one son. Girls are a nightmare. At least, I know I could be when I was their age," she added, laughing along with the others. I laughed a little, too, but I didn't really feel it.

"She'll get over it," Evelyn promised. "I'm not saying the girls are exactly easy right now, but they have tremendously mellowed since they hit seventeen. Like they cleared a hurdle or something."

"Can you believe this is our life?" Olivia asked as she swirled her wine in her glass, gazing at the table where our daughters sat. "Sitting around at lunch, talking about the kids. We used to be young. We used to have fun. That's what I need," she decided.

"What, going to a swanky affair on New Year's Eve isn't your idea of fun?" I asked.

"That's just it, though. Don't get me wrong, I enjoy getting fixed up and doing something special. But it's still so…"

"Mature?" I ventured, and she nodded hard. "I know. I get the feeling that if we tried to go out to a bar or a club today, we would leave humiliated."

"If I had to go to a bar or a club today," Evelyn joked, "I have to head home by nine at the latest."

We all laughed knowingly. "Maybe we can talk the hunkholes into investing in a club for the middle-aged," Olivia suggested. "We can play all the music we used to listen to when we were young, we could wear flat shoes if we wanted to, and we could go home in time for a cup of tea and a true crime documentary. I'd be their biggest customer."

The change in topic brightened the mood, and

we were all laughing and making plans by the time our food arrived. Evelyn was right. They all were. The more personally I took Sienna's behavior, the harder I would cling and the harder she would push me away. Another glass of wine and a slice of spinach quiche went a long way toward loosening me up until I was genuinely looking forward to the afternoon by the time we stood and got our things together.

"Hello, ladies! It's so good to see you out here!" Grace Schwartz was all smiles as she approached our table with Penelope close behind. "Getting some last-minute shopping done today?" she asked while zipping up a faux fur jacket.

"No matter how I tell myself to stick to a list, I always end up going overboard in the last week," Pepper confessed, and we all laughed, nodding in agreement.

"I think I should wait until the last week," Evelyn decided. "This way, I won't lose track of everything I bought right after Halloween, telling myself I wanted to get a jump on it."

We all laughed again except for Penelope, staring at the girls' table. A glance in that direction revealed something interesting. Sienna wouldn't look at her. It was like she went out of her way not to, keeping her head low, her eyes on the floor. They weren't even in the same grade.

"Lourde, Olivia, I understand there's a chance you could be working at our new hotel." Grace was nothing but smiles, and she looked back and forth between us. "Is that true? It would be so much fun having the two of you around."

"Do you have the inside scoop?" Olivia asked, and somehow, she even managed to sound playful when I knew she was anything but. She wanted this even more than I did. I was ambitious, sure, but she was ferocious. We worked well together.

"Oh, please," Grace insisted, laughing gently as a blush touched her cheeks. "I don't mean to tell secrets. But to be honest with you, I've been talking with my brother about it," she explained, looking back to where the man in question now wound his way between tables, coming toward us. She leaned in a little, winking. "Between us, he made it sound like you have the edge. Good luck."

There was no chance to absorb this before he reached us. "Hello, ladies." Kelvin shone his warm smile over the group. "It's so good to see you."

Maybe it was the fact that I was a woman. Maybe I was a little more sensitive to him, the way he acted because I had spent my life gritting my teeth and smiling when I really wanted to tell somebody to fuck off. That was what I wanted to tell him to do, point-blank, no sugarcoating it.

And it was exactly what I couldn't do if I wanted Alex Schwartz's business. I had to play nice, be friendly, and act like I didn't notice the way it always seemed like he was in on a joke whenever our eyes met. Like there was some unearned intimacy between us.

"We were just on our way out," I explained, though that much was obvious considering we were putting our coats on. Really, the timing couldn't have been better. I shuddered to think of being trapped, forced to spend time with him.

"You know, for what it's worth," he murmured, leaning in a little and lowering his voice. "I hope you and your partner end up decorating the hotel."

"Let's put some of that positive energy into the world." It was getting harder to smile my way through my discomfort. He stood too close and looked down at me with a light in his eyes that made my skin crawl.

"Well, not to overstate my importance..." He lowered his head further until his mouth almost brushed my ear. "I do have a significant amount of influence here. I would be happy to push your name to the top of the pile of potential decorators. I've seen enough from you to know you would be the ideal choice."

I craned my neck in a vain attempt at putting space between us. "I didn't know you were familiar with our work."

His gray eyes twinkled. "Who says I was talking about your work?"

"Uncle Kelvin? Are we going?" Penelope offered me a brief, polite smile from beside her uncle.

"Of course. I don't wanna hold you guys up." He chuckled indulgently, turning back toward me. "Don't you worry," he murmured with a wink. "It's in the bag. All you have to do is draw up your plans." His eyes traveled over me again as he added, "You have no idea how much I'm looking forward to it."

I was going to need a very long, very hot shower by the time we returned to the cabin. There was so much commotion happening all at once that it didn't seem like anyone noticed our conversation, not even Olivia, who was in the middle of a conversation with Rose. There was too much action and movement, but I was glad for that. The whole thing was uncomfortable enough without hearing pointed questions.

The most pointed questions would've come from Barrett. I could only thank God he wasn't there to witness Kelvin's shameless flirting. For the first time since we found out Alex Schwartz was looking for a decorator, a pit of uncertainty settled in my gut. Was it really such a good idea to compete for this opportunity? Was it worth it if it meant being forced to spend time with somebody who made my skin crawl? I didn't think he would ever go any further than that, but then, did he have to?

Was I seriously trying to talk myself out of how I felt? It was enough that he made me uneasy. I didn't need to wait until he took things too far. But how would I explain my feelings to Olivia? She was one of my closest, oldest friends, but she also owned fifty percent of our business. My decision would affect her.

So much for my good mood. "What happened to my scarf?" I asked, looking under my chair for it, then under the table. "It was here, over the back of my chair."

Pepper looked around, shrugging. "Hmm, I didn't see it." The girls helped, but it was soon clear the delicate, cashmere scarf was gone. One more thing to nag in the back of my mind as we left the restaurant.

4

BARRETT

"Remember what I said." It wasn't enough for Pepper to threaten her husband alone. Oh, no. She had to glare at each of us in turn—Ari, Magnus, and me. She then turned that glare onto Colton, Noah, and Evan.

"Mom," Lucian groaned. "It's going to be fine."

"You broke your arm in Vermont last winter," she reminded him with a scowl.

"Somehow, he lived to ski another day." Connor placed his hands on her shoulders, smiling as he added, "Let him be a kid."

"He'll be fine," I reassured her on our way out of the cabin. Lourde shook her head, chuckling, taking Pepper by the hand and leading her back to the kitchen, where she and the other women were having coffee. They had decided to spend the earlier part of the day wrapping gifts and baking cookies. The idea of coming back to a cabin that smelled like cinnamon, sugar, and chocolate wasn't half bad.

"Don't worry, Lucian," Colton joked as we split up into our respective SUVs. "We won't get you in trouble with mommy."

His laughter died a quick death when he caught me watching, like I wasn't supposed to hear him teasing his cousin. I waited until we were in the vehicle before asking, "Was that necessary?"

"Oh, come on, Dad." He had the nerve to look over his shoulder to where Evan sat behind me. "I was just screwing around. You bust balls with Uncle Connor all the time."

"Busting balls is one thing. You're being cruel."

He rolled his eyes and scoffed, looking out the passenger side window. "It's not my fault he's younger. For Christ's sake." He was lucky Evan was with us. I didn't want to embarrass him in front of his friend.

Somehow, I stayed quiet on the way to the resort, a short drive up the road, where the practically over-flowing parking lot told me how many people would already be on the slopes. There we were, trying to get an early start. But this was the busiest time of year out here, as well. It made me think of all the business Alex would do this time next year when the hotel was open. He was less than five minutes down the road from one of the most popular ski resorts in the area. It was sheer luck, the way he was able to snap up the property when it went up for sale.

By the time we found parking spots, there was a light snowfall. The boys got the equipment together and trailed behind us as we made our way to the lodge, strung up with garland, lights, and displaying wreaths in every window. It was a festive scene that helped lift my spirits a little. I hadn't been able to get Kelvin off my mind since running into him a couple of days back.

Lourde had been in such a good mood since we left the hotel that day, excited about the potential for working on such a big project, excited about the holiday, that I didn't have the heart to bring him up no matter how determined I was at dinner our first night. Was there a way I could wait until after the new year to express my discomfort? Would it be too late by then?

"That's why these old guys wanted to bring us along for skiing," Noah joked. "So we could carry the equipment because they're too frail."

"You better watch your mouth," Ari warned with a smirk. "I might be your father, but I am a couple of decades away from being a broken-down old man."

"Yeah?" Noah taunted good-naturedly. "Then how about we see who's fastest out there? Fathers against sons. Evan, you could race Magnus," he suggested.

"What does the winning side get?" Evan asked.

"Not having to carry the equipment back across a mile-long parking lot?" Lucian suggested.

"No, we need more than that," Colton decided.

"Losers have to cook dinner?" Evan asked.

Connor laughed over his shoulder. "Right. That would be a great idea if we all wanted food poisoning because we all know who's going to win. It won't be you, boys."

"Have you ever cooked a meal?" I asked Colton, who, of course, rolled his eyes and snickered. "No, I don't think that would be a good idea."

After a little more bickering, we agreed the losers should treat the winners to lunch at the restaurant inside the lodge. "I'm looking forward to the burger I'm going to eat on your dime," Noah announced to his father.

Ari only scoffed. "As if you haven't been eating out on my dime your entire life," he retorted. "Or did you think your allowance magically appears in your bank account?"

The energy was friendly but competitive by the time we got in line for the lifts. Connor stood next to me and nudged me with his elbow. "Can you imagine ever doing anything like this with my dad?" he asked, snickering as he adjusted his goggles. "These boys don't understand how good they have it with us."

No, they didn't understand. Neither did Connor, really. But there was no way to explain to a person that having an overbearing, demanding father was a far cry from the hell Evelyn and I grew up in. When I was Colton's age, I would've killed for a father who gave a damn about me.

No, my son would never understand how good he had it. And in a way, I was glad for that. I wanted him to know the world and be a decent man, but some things he didn't need to experience. I had kept all of that ugly shit away from him and Sienna.

"Okay," Magnus called out once we were at the top of the slope. The scene was picturesque, to put it mildly, like something off a postcard. Trees were dusted with snow that continued falling at a steady clip while snowy peaks rose above them. Smoke curled up from the chimneys down at the lodge.

I took a moment to enjoy it before stepping up and grinning at my son. "What do you say?" I asked.

He chuckled, shrugging. "I don't know, old man. Do you think you have what it takes?"

I did like his confidence. He would need it if there was any hope of making his own path in the world. "I don't have to think," I replied, shrugging like he did. "Besides, I'm too busy imagining the lunch you're going to owe me."

The little fucker laughed, then took off without me. What a shame for him that my reflexes weren't as slow as he thought they would be since I was on the move a heartbeat later while knowing laughter rose up behind me. Instead of staying focused on his black ski suit ahead of me, I focused on the lodge. I wasn't trying to catch him. I was trying to reach the lodge. A very distinct difference in mindset.

He might've shouted something when I passed him, but I was too busy leaving him in the cloud of fresh powder coming up from my skis. There was nothing like this feeling, the freedom, the icy air hitting my lungs. There were few times in my life I felt this alive.

What made it even better was coming around to a stop at the bottom of the slope, waiting for Colton to catch up. To his credit, it didn't take more than a few seconds, but it was more than enough for my victory to be undisputed. "I was starting to think you lost your way," I said, laughing when he scowled. "Looks like your cheating was for nothing."

One by one, the pairs of skiers made it to where we waited. And in every race, the boys were trounced. The finish between Magnus and Evan was the closest, but even then, there was no contest. "Looks like I still got it!" Magnus crowed, high-fiving Ari.

"Maybe you kids should reconsider writing checks you can't cash," Connor joked. "But it was a nice effort. Really, good for you." Sarcasm dripped from his voice.

"I'm going back up," Lucian grumbled, followed by the rest of the boys. Magnus and Ari trailed behind them, and they weren't exactly trying to be quiet as they recounted their winning runs down the slope.

I would have followed them and joined in if it wasn't for someone calling out to me. I turned with a sinking heart to find Kelvin Barnes strolling out of the lodge with a shit-eating grin plastered to his face. "Barrett Black. What are the chances? It seems like we're destined to keep running into each other this holiday season."

"Kelvin," I replied curtly because that was all he deserved. "Do you know my brother-in-law, Connor?"

Kelvin turned to him with the same empty smile. "Of course. I can't imagine anyone not knowing who Connor Diamond is. I see the family resemblance between you and your sister," he added while his smile widened.

Motherfucker. He had to find a way to bring Lourde into the conversation. "See you around," I offered, ready to be the bigger man. He was nothing. Another piece of shit who thought he had what it took to lure my wife away from me. Like that was fucking possible. He wasn't worth wasting time on. I had already given him enough of my mental space the past two days as it was. The distraction of those races with the boys made something abundantly clear. I had a much better time when Kelvin was the furthest thing from my thoughts.

That wasn't enough for him. "By the way," Kelvin added before I could get out of his presence. "I ran into your wife yesterday and ended up with her scarf. Pale blue, like somebody made it by hand? It's in my car," he explained with a laugh and a shrug. "I can go get it for you if you want."

If only he hadn't described the scarf Lourde was

wearing yesterday morning before she went out shopping. "What are you getting at?" I barked. To hell with diplomacy. "You're telling me my wife was with you yesterday? Is that what this is about?"

"Easy, easy." He backed up two steps, his hands raised like this was all innocent. "I shouldn't have brought it up, I guess. I thought I was being helpful."

The idyllic holiday scene around me went red. Blood red, like the blood now pounding in my head and roaring in my ears. "Listen to me," I gritted out, barely aware of Connor taking me by the arm like he wanted to hold me back. "You do not speak of my wife. Understand? Is that getting through your skull?"

"Calm down," Kelvin laughed. "Trouble in paradise, Barrett? Otherwise, why would you fly into a rage like this?"

"Let's go," Connor muttered, glaring at him while pulling me away. "This trash isn't worth it."

"I'm going to fucking kill that guy." It still seemed like a fairly strong option from where I was standing, as I looked over my shoulder to find Kelvin shaking his head, chuckling.

"Then find a way to fucking kill him that doesn't involve your son being here along with hundreds of witnesses," Connor muttered. He had a point.

Drastic measures aside, it wouldn't do me any favors to get caught up in a fistfight. I had a reputation to think of.

One thing I could not think of was skiing. I'd be damned if I spent another minute there, knowing Kelvin was there too. "I'm going back to the cabin," I decided. "Can you take Colton and Evan back with you?"

"Are you sure that's what you want to do?" Connor tipped his head to the side, wincing. "We barely got started."

"I need to talk to Lourde, and it can't wait."

"Hang on." He folded his arms, his head snapping back. "You don't think she would—"

"I'm not having this conversation." No, I didn't believe she would give that man the time of day, but I had questions like how the man ended up with her scarf, for starters. She hadn't spoken a word about running into him yesterday. Was she trying to keep it a secret? It didn't look good either way.

I was unsure of a lot of things as I headed for the parking lot, but one fact was abundantly clear.

We were going to get to the bottom of this.

5

———

LOURDE

When we reached the cabin after an afternoon at the spa, I felt like a new woman. My muscles were loose after a two-hour massage which it turned out I desperately needed. My cheeks tingled after a facial, my toes freshly pedicured, and my nails shimmered thanks to a fresh coat of dark red varnish tipped with gold glitter.

"All things considered, I think we made the right decision today," I announced as we stepped into the warm space that was such a welcome change from the icy air outside. The others nodded their agreement, looking relieved and refreshed.

Sliding out of my coat, I looked around the living room. There was a fire burning in the hearth, but nobody around to enjoy it. The plate of fresh cookies we'd left on the coffee table before leaving for the spa looked untouched. "They're not back yet?" I asked, meaning our guys and the boys.

"Magnus just texted," Evelyn announced, holding up her phone. "They decided on a rematch after lunch, whatever that means. He said they should be back soon."

That didn't explain why one of the SUVs was parked in front of the cabin. I would've gotten a heads-up if someone were sick or injured, right? I texted Barrett on my way up the stairs, intending to get changed.

ME: *Everything ok?*

I HAD BARELY SENT the message when a faint ping coming from the direction of our bedroom startled me. Had he left his phone here? I trotted down the hall, more concerned than ever.

"Honey? Are you here?" Opening the bedroom door, I found my husband seated in front of the fireplace. Flames crackled merrily and warmed up the room while the light played off his chiseled features.

He was a brooding prince, with anger simmering just below the surface.

He hadn't shown any indication of hearing me come in. "Hello?" I murmured, slowly approaching the sofa where Barrett sat with one arm stretched across the top and a half-empty glass of scotch in his hand. "What happened? Why are you in here alone?" I asked.

"I'm going to ask you a question." Yes, he was angry, though I had no idea why. It hung heavy in his voice, clipping his words. "And I want the truth. Don't hold anything back because you think I don't want to hear it."

"You're making me nervous."

"There's no reason to be nervous." That was easy for him to say. He wasn't the one who'd just walked in on an interrogation. "Just answer. Did you see Kelvin yesterday?"

I should've known. Whatever this was, he had to be behind it somewhere. There was no other reason for my husband to speak to me through gritted teeth. "Yes, I did." I stood next to the sofa, wanting to sit but thinking it might be better to leave some distance between us. The energy in the room was tense and getting worse by the moment.

"Were you going to ever tell me about it?"

"I didn't know I had to." I stood up straighter because I was not in the wrong here. "Should I prepare a daily statement on everyone I've exchanged a word with?"

"Don't," he warned. Finally, he tore his attention away from the blazing fire and looked at me. Normally, the intensity in his stare would've turned me on. This was not one of those times. "You realize the fact that you didn't mention it makes it seem like you were trying to cover something up. I looked like a smacked ass out there, which was exactly what he was going for."

"What happened?" I asked. "What set all of this in motion? What did he tell you?"

"Was there anything for him to tell me?"

"*Goddammit,* Barrett," I growled out. He wasn't the only one who could get growly when he was pissed. "That's enough. If you think I'm trying to hide some little affair with a slug like him, I don't know whether to laugh or cry. Don't you know me better than that by now?"

"I don't think you would do that," he admitted, groaning. "Honestly, I don't know what the hell I think right now except for one thing. I don't want you around him. *Ever.*"

"It's not that simple, and we both know it." When

he growled this time, I stepped up in front of him. "You know it isn't. We both have to exist in the world, right? We both have to grind our teeth and pretend to smile when we would rather do anything but. Please, don't act like you don't know how it works. You mean to tell me you've never had to politely disengage when a woman tried to hit on you if it meant keeping the business relationship afloat?"

"You know how important this is to me, and you would still choose your business?"

"Now it's your turn to stop bullshitting me." His brows lifted, but he said nothing. "You know damn well I'm not going to give up trying to land this project because of him. And honestly, I can't believe you would ask me to. You think I don't keep you in mind? You think I haven't been wrestling with myself since yesterday, wondering if I should tell you how uncomfortable he made me?"

He sat forward, belting back the scotch and leaving the glass on the end table. "What did he do?"

"It's impossible to describe. You would have to be in the situation yourself. He never touched me or anything like that, and he never comes right out and says what he means, but I know. We ran into him with Grace and Penelope Schwartz at lunch yester-day, and he went out of his way to flirt. That's it."

"How did he end up with your scarf?"

My eyes closed before I released a sigh. "I should've known he did it. He grabbed it off the back of my chair when I wasn't looking. It was hectic, with everybody getting ready to leave all at once. It went missing, and I told myself someone picked it up in passing at the restaurant, but I should've known it was him." Looking back, I added, "He had a shopping bag in one hand. He must've shoved the scarf inside."

"Gotcha. That makes sense if you put yourself inside his sick mind for a minute." He was loosening up, moving his mouth when he spoke instead of forcing everything out through clenched teeth—a good sign. "For what it's worth," he offered. "It's not that I don't trust you. You know I do, implicitly. I don't trust him."

"I know, but I can handle myself."

"Lourde..." He sighed.

"Barrett," I retorted. "I can. I'm not some innocent babe in the woods." Still, I felt nothing but dread when I imagined the possibility of seeing Kelvin around the hotel. "Alex could still decide to go in another direction. I'll play nice until that time comes, but if we get the job, all bets are off. Let me handle this," I urged when he rolled his eyes and looked away. "Can you please trust me? I'm not trying to convince you I'll stay faithful. You know I would. Trust my intelligence. I'm not a child."

His heavy sigh told me he was coming around. "I know you aren't. But you can't expect me to stand back and watch you be preyed on. Not if there's anything I can do to stop it."

"And I love you for that," I said, sinking to my knees in front of him, looking up at him with a smile. He reached down and stroked my hair before cupping my cheek.

"Your skin is so soft," he murmured, gliding with his thumb above my jawline.

"I just got a facial." And then he snorted because no matter how old he got, there would always be part of him that was still a teenage boy. "Ha ha," I muttered with a roll of my eyes that made him laugh. Kelvin was in the past for now, something I couldn't have been happier about.

"Well, it works for you," he decided. "What did you do today?"

"I also had a massage. I didn't realize how stiff I was." And I had no doubt Kelvin played a big part in that. That slimy son of a bitch. Thinking he could manipulate us so easily. Like Barrett would ever believe I spent a minute of time with Kelvin that wasn't absolutely mandatory. It was sad.

"You're feeling nice and loose?" he asked, a knowing smile played over his mouth. "Sorry, but you know I can't have you in this position without thinking along those lines, Dollface."

"You mean on my knees in front of you?" I questioned innocently, parting his legs and running my hands up his thighs. "Did you do any skiing at all?" I asked, sinking my fingers into his muscles as I traveled upward.

"A little. Maybe I could use a massage…"

"You think so?" My hands traveled higher, and he sucked in a breath that ended on a soft moan once my thumbs stroked his zipper and what was underneath it.

"I know so," he grunted, slouching a little until his ass slid across the cushion closer to me. "There is one part of me that's starting to ache, for sure."

"Hmm… it does feel pretty stiff," I observed, clicking my tongue in false concern. "I might need to get to the bottom of this."

He chuckled softly once my palm ran over his growing bulge. "By all means."

Glancing up from his crotch, I shared a brief grin with him, then began lowering his zipper.

"I might need a lot of extra attention." He reached out to pluck at my cashmere sweater. "And you might need to do this topless. It can't hurt, right?"

"Whatever my client needs." I had to giggle, though, as I lifted the sweater over my head then removed my bra, he stared hard, watching my every move. "I never thought I would play the role of the masseuse offering happy endings."

While I unbuckled his belt, he stroked my breasts, thumbing my nipples. The playfulness ended, replaced by a heat much greater than what I felt at my back from the fireplace. He lifted his hips, and I slid his slacks down to his ankles, taking his boxer briefs with them. It didn't matter how many times we did this. I would always feel the same stirring of hunger once his proud, rigid erection sprang free.

The hunger was enough to make me descend on him all at once, taking him deep in my mouth instead of teasing him like I originally intended. This was what I needed. This connection. The reminder of what mattered. Not Kelvin or anyone else outside this room, right now.

We had each other, and I needed him like I needed air. I would never have eyes for anybody but him, and I would never want anything more than this. Bringing him pleasure, making him forget everything beyond the touch of my tongue along his shaft, swirling around the ridge of his mushroom head to taste his salty precum until he groaned and buried his hands in my hair.

"Mmm. Fuck," he whispered, moving his hips, thrusting himself farther into my mouth. I had been in this position enough times that relaxing my throat and taking him deeper was second nature by now. He released a throaty growl, clamping a hand on the back of my head that sent a jolt straight to my pussy.

"Fuck, yes," he grunted out, breathing faster. I let that breathing guide me, followed the way it hitched and sped up whenever I hit just the right spot. "Fuck, you're always so good at sucking my cock. You know just what to do."

For him, only for him. He needed to know that. I added to the sensation, moaning when he did. He didn't have to lay a finger on me to get me wet. The sound of his pleasure never failed to heighten mine. My slit was a river by the time he went from panting to grunting and groaning.

"You ready, baby. Shi-it, that's it. You gonna swallow my cum?" I moaned again, and he grunted louder, fucking my face as he lost his control. "Yes...

just like that, don't stop... fuck, Dollface, I'm coming!"

The first blast hit the back of my throat, and I greedily swallowed before he filled my mouth again and again. His legs were shaking by the time he finished, and I let him carefully slip from between my pursed lips. His head fell back against the cushions as he sighed deeply, and the sound made my pussy throb.

"How are you feeling now?" I asked, rubbing his thighs again, smirking up at him while he fought to compose himself. I did that to him. I was sort of proud of myself.

He managed to chuckle between ragged breaths, sitting up with a light in his eyes that made my clit ache for his touch. "I'm feeling like I need to return the favor."

Like I would ever stop him from doing that.

BARRETT

"What's wrong with Mom? Is she sick?" Sienna's sudden, unexpected question caught me off guard.

It was two days until Christmas, the day after I almost beat the shit out of Kelvin Barnes in front of the holiday tourists in Vail. Lourde and I had made up, not that we were fighting, but we cleared the air yesterday.

I still carried lingering, residual guilt when I woke up this morning. I shouldn't have approached it that way, looking back at how nervous she was, like a deer in headlights after what Kelvin had already put her through. I had no right to do that. The fact that she even considered putting my dick in her mouth after I confronted her was one more example of how completely perfect she was.

Now, while setting up a tray to take up to Lourde, I gave my daughter what I hoped was a reassuring chuckle. "She's fine. I thought I would bring her breakfast in bed, that's all."

"Oh, okay." She munched a piece of toast, her phone in the other hand the way it always was. "Aria and Valentina want to go skiing today."

"You should go with them, get some exercise. Get a little color in your cheeks, too," I added, patting her cheek as I passed her at the breakfast nook tucked into one corner of the kitchen.

"I don't know. I think I might just hang out here."

Nobody would ever call me the perfect father. If they did, I'd have to laugh in their face. It wasn't that I didn't try. Colton and Sienna were everything that mattered besides their mother, and I gave them everything I could. There were always times, though, when it wasn't enough.

Now, I stopped midway through pouring Lourde a cup of coffee and gave Sienna my full attention. "Is there anything you want to talk about?" I asked. There were footsteps overhead, voices. We wouldn't be alone for long. Would she stall until there was no chance of getting a straight answer?

Her head snapped up from the screen. So that was all it took to get her full attention? I would have to make a note of it. "No?"

"Is that a question or an answer?"

She rolled her eyes, sighing. "No. There's nothing."

I didn't believe her, but I knew she would double down if I said anything. If there was one thing my daughter had inherited from me, it was her talent for digging her heels in. "All right. Well, I'm here if you want to talk. Maybe we can catch up. You can tell me all about your new favorite dolls," I suggested.

The kid came damn close to gagging. "Dolls? Dad, come on."

"What, you don't play with dolls anymore?" It was only when I snickered that she rolled her eyes again and groaned.

"You're about five years too late," she informed me in a voice dripping with pity.

"I know you don't think I pay attention," I added as I lifted the tray from the counter. "But there are some things I know, sweetheart. As for skiing, you do whatever it is you want to do." There was a twinge of guilt reverberating in my chest as I left the kitchen, but if anything, she looked relieved to see me go.

"Breakfast in bed?" Evelyn asked when we

crossed paths in the upstairs hallway while she was on her way out of her bedroom. "Lucky lady. I wish my husband would do nice things for me," she added, raising her voice and turning her head toward the bedroom door for Magnus to hear. I was chuckling by the time I balanced the tray on one knee so I could open our door farther down the hall.

Lourde must have heard us talking in the hallway because she was in the process of sitting up when she found me entering with a loaded tray. "Oh, wow! What is all this?" she asked, propping herself up with pillows wedged between her back and the padded headboard.

"I was thinking you might extend that relaxing trend you started yesterday," I explained while balancing the tray across her knees. "So I put a little something together for you this morning."

She looked down at the yogurt parfait, toast, and the latte I'd prepared the way she liked it. "This is terrific. Thank you so much." A long, lingering kiss was my reward, along with the little smile she wore when she pulled back. "I was just lying here, looking out the window. Isn't it gorgeous?"

"I don't know. I like this view better." Sitting on the edge of the bed, I tucked a strand of silky, dark hair behind her ear. "But yes, it's beautiful out there."

I turned my head to take in the sight of the snow coming down in big flakes that almost painted the sky white. "There is nothing like standing outside in the middle of a snowfall like this," I mused. "When the whole world is so quiet."

"Do you remember that one Christmas when we had all that snow?" she asked between sips of latte. "It was Sienna's first Christmas, wasn't it?"

The memory stirred my heart. Thinking about them when they were so young. "It was a good thing we decided not to travel that year and have Christmas at home," I mused. "We could've gotten stuck on the way to the airport with all those other drivers. What a way to spend the holiday."

Her fond smile widened. "But then we took them to Central Park once the streets were cleared. Remember pulling them on the sled?"

"I remember you trying to go down that one slope with Colton in your lap." I laughed at the memory of the two of them tumbling off the sled, with Lourde landing in a snowdrift. The image of her sputtering face was still clear, along with Colton's high-pitched laughter.

"It's not funny!" Though she was laughing too.

"That was a good day. It was a good Christmas too. Quiet, simple."

"Simple? You weren't the one up half the night setting up that indoor jungle gym. And I put that tricycle together," I added. "I earned my dad stripes that Christmas Eve."

Her knee tapped my back. "If I gave you the chance to do that again, would you turn me down?"

That was easy. "I would go back in a heartbeat." I turned away from the window to find her smiling a little sadly now, her eyes shining. "But..." I continued, rubbing her leg through the duvet covering it. "One season ends, another starts. There are good things in both."

"I just feel like... they don't need me anymore." She set down her spoon, then set the tray aside after having eaten around half of what I brought up. "To be honest, that's part of the reason why this project with Alex Schwartz is such a big deal for me. I mean, Olivia wants it, too," she elaborated. "But from my point of view, aside from it being a great opportunity, I think I need something to take the place of being needed."

"Let me tell you something." I leaned in, one arm on either side of her. I wanted to be close so there was no chance of misunderstanding. "There will never be a time when they don't need you, and never, ever, will there be a day when *I* don't need you. You have to remember that."

"I know." I could hear it in her voice—it wasn't the same.

"All right, so the kids have gotten older. There's a new normal. That's a good thing." When she scoffed gently, I added, "Would you rather they be completely dependent upon us for the rest of their lives?"

"Of course not," she replied without hesitation.

"Same here. But how does the old saying go? When you pray for rain, you've got to deal with the mud too."

A smirk played over her mouth. "Listen to you. The billionaire philosopher."

"I'm a Renaissance man." We were both chuckling as I leaned in, catching her mouth, where the taste of strawberry jelly and vanilla yogurt lingered.

"I'll tell you one thing," I added between kisses, moving closer as she wrapped her arms around my shoulders. "Nobody would ever believe you're the mother of two teenagers. No way."

"Oh, please," she whispered. Her breath touched my ear and awakened my endless need for her. The need to touch, taste, claim.

"Are you serious?" My lips skimmed the tops of her firm tits. They hadn't changed much, either. "You don't look a day older than you did at our wedding."

"The things you'll say just to get into my panties..."

Her teasing laughter was cut short by the touch of my hand under the duvet, creeping up her thigh. "Please," I reminded her in a growl. "I haven't needed to talk my way into your panties... *ever.*"

My scalp tangled once her fingers began moving through my hair. "Okay, you have a point there," she whispered. Her head fell back against the pillow once my fingers crept higher under her nightgown, skimming the silky skin leading up to her firm, ripe ass.

"Hang on." I stopped in the middle of licking my way up her throat. "I have a better idea." For a few seconds, I made myself busy, tossing pillows and bedding on the floor in front of the crackling hearth, then turned back to my bride. She squealed when I picked her up out of bed and carried her to the makeshift bed I'd created in front of the fire.

"I like this," she whispered, gazing up at me with her hair fanned across the silk pillowcase, rich brown against cream. Her blue eyes shone in the firelight, and her skin glowed. Her nipples stood out against the silky nightgown that so perfectly molded itself to her every curve. She was a wet dream come to life, and she was all mine.

"Do you, Dollface?" On my knees beside her, I leaned down and covered her mouth with mine. The first stroke of my tongue stirred a moan in her throat that went straight to my dick, standing it at attention.

Now, all that stood between her body and my skillful touch was that thin nightgown, which I slid from her calf to her knee and halfway up her thigh while we kissed slowly, with nothing and no one on our minds but each other at this moment.

How was it possible she still excited me so much after so many years together? How many men in my position got tired of their wives and decided they could do better? I was lucky. I was smart enough to know I could never do better than her because there wasn't anything better in the world.

"Oh, Barrett," she moaned into my mouth when I found the source of the heat radiating from between her thighs.

"This pussy... will be the death of me." Her pussy was soaked, stirring my desire. I had to be inside that heat.

We both groaned when I worked two digits inside her. There was something so familiar about this, but it somehow felt like the first time. The sounds of her growing pleasure never failed to make my heart race. She had a way of giving herself over completely, sinking into the sensation brought to life by my hands, my mouth.

"So good," she whimpered. "God, it feels so good. Right there!" she begged when I rubbed against her inner wall. Her hips moved in slow, sensual circles.

I was going to come in my pants if this went on much longer. Watching her body move to the rhythm I set. Feeling her inching closer to the edge, the way she changed. Tightening around my fingers. The flush that crept over her chest.

Her nipple was too close to my mouth to resist. I lapped at it through the thin fabric, grazed it with my teeth until she bucked and whined, and finally came with a final jerk of her hips. "God, yes! Yes, Barrett!" she whispered, riding it out, prolonging it the way I wanted.

I couldn't wait much longer. There was a wet spot growing on the front of my boxer briefs, which I took off along with my pajama pants before rolling onto my side and facing her. She was still dazed by the time I turned her to face me, draping her leg over my hip.

"This is perfect," she whispered with a soft smile after pulling off my T-shirt.

"You're perfect." No fabric in existence could compete with the silk of her skin. I feasted on it once the nightgown was tossed aside, using my hands and mouth to indulge while she guided me inside her.

"Yes..." Her head fell back on the first stroke. She was still clenching and squeezing after her orgasm, and I was caught between wanting to ride the wave and let her milk me and wanting this to last forever.

I chose the latter, going slow, concentrating on every inch I penetrated her, every inch of skin I caressed. Every sigh, whimper, every time my name tumbled from her lips in a moan.

We had barely finished coming in each other's arms when I knew we were going nowhere this morning. I wasn't about to waste a minute of this. "I hope you didn't have plans until the afternoon," I whispered, brushing strands of hair away from her flushed cheek. "Because I'm going to need a second round."

She quirked an eyebrow. "Only a second round? And there I was, hoping for a third."

I always loved a challenge.

7

LOURDE

"What do you mean you're going out tonight?" I couldn't hide my disappointment at Colton's offhand announcement on his way out the door late Christmas Eve morning. He, Noah, and Evan looked pretty sure of themselves like their plans were set in stone.

Colton lifted a shoulder. "We'll be around to go to dinner, but then a few guys from school whose families are out here wanted to hang out. It's not like we're going to miss any of the family holiday stuff or whatever it is."

I couldn't hide how that hurt me. It wasn't what he said, but the way he said it. So dismissive. "I realize it is a huge sacrifice for you to spend time with your family during the holidays," I murmured. "But you don't have to make it sound like it's torture, you know."

His face fell because, at the end of the day, he was not a bad kid. Just a little too full of himself sometimes, which was exactly why he and Barrett butted heads like they did. They were too alike. "It's not torture. I didn't make it sound that way," he grumbled. "It's not like we'll be out all night. I'll be the first one down the stairs to see what Santa brought."

"I'm hoping he brought you a little humility to go in your stocking."

"Humility." He narrowed his eyes and pursed his lips thoughtfully. "Is it Bergdorf who carries that, or Nordstrom? I can't remember."

"You better get out of here," I warned with a smile, giving him a little shove. Noah and the other boys were waiting for him outside, all of them intending on walking down to the village for lunch with their friends and the promise of picking up a couple of gifts. Typical teenage boys. Waiting until the last minute.

Not me. I could never. All of the rushing around was done. All that was left was soaking in the holiday spirit after a much-too-heavy breakfast of biscuits and gravy, fried eggs, cinnamon rolls, and countless other sinful foods. I could have easily drifted into a food coma, but I decided to caffeinate myself instead.

As I entered the kitchen, planning on making another latte, I caught Olivia in the middle of a whispered conversation with Ari. "I just want to know, either way," she insisted. "Whether he wants us or not. I can't stand the unknown." Ari was rubbing her shoulders while she fretted, and the look she gave me spoke volumes about her tension.

"We'll find out when we find out," I reminded her as evenly as I could. "We aren't the only people dying to decorate that property. It's only fair that he would want to weigh his options."

She scowled. "Yes, and he'll keep us dangling like this. It would be nice to go into the new year with an answer. That's all I'm saying."

"I understand. I feel the same way." I looked at Ari, feeling a little helpless. As far as I was concerned, he could bail me out at any time.

"I know this seems like a make-or-break deal," he offered. "But it's not. You have more than enough work to keep you both busy, and your network is expanding all the time. If the answer is no, this is hardly the end of the road."

"I know." Still, she chewed her lip, frowning, folding her arms as she leaned against the counter. "I just wish I knew for sure. That's all. I don't like question marks hanging over my head."

Neither did I. I especially didn't like wondering if, should we get the job, Kelvin had anything to do with it. I was ready to assume he was exaggerating about putting a good word in and using his influence, but what if he wasn't? I didn't want to think we only got the work because he wanted to sleep with me. The idea made me crave a scalding shower.

Eventually, the topic changed, with all of us hanging around the cabin and spending a quiet day. The men played cards for a while. I sat down with a jigsaw puzzle, which Evelyn helped me with. Olivia and Pepper read by the fire, drinking hot chocolate spiked with a little peppermint schnapps.

It wasn't bad, but I wanted to keep a clear head because there was one last errand I had to run. The owner of the jewelry store told me to come by after three o'clock after the last delivery of specialized gifts would arrive from their workshop. I would pick up Barrett's watch and Sienna's earrings now that she wouldn't be there to witness me making the purchase.

It was a quarter to three when I got up and

grabbed my purse and coat. Barrett was now playing chess with Connor. The two of them couldn't have looked any more like something out of a menswear ad in their cords and cable knit sweaters, poised over the board between them, a plate of cookies off to the side and cups of mulled wine from a pot kept warm on the stove all day. "Where are you headed?" he asked when he noticed me.

"I'm just running down to the village to pick up something." I buttoned my coat and pulled a knit hat over my head. "I'll be back in no time."

He arched an eyebrow, giving me a suspicious look as he stood to meet me at the door. "What are you picking up?"

I stood on tiptoe to give him a brief kiss. "Santa needed me to step in for him on a couple things. Looks like you made the Nice List, after all."

A growl stirred in his throat, and as usual, it had the power to make my skin tingle. "Damn. I'll have to try twice as hard to make the naughty list next year."

"Well, if you need any help..." I ducked out of the way when he made a grab for me, giggling on my way to the front door. "Your reflexes are getting slow, Black. You might wanna work on that."

"Here's hoping Santa decided to give me a time

machine for Christmas so I can turn back the clock." We were both laughing as I left, stepping into what passed for an absolutely idyllic Christmas Eve afternoon. There was a light snow falling by the time I got behind the wheel of one of the SUVs. I would have walked, but the jewelry store was running on a shortened schedule for the holiday, and I wanted to get there before they closed.

It was clear as I approached the village that I wasn't the only one crossing a few last items off their shopping list today. The energy in the air was unmatched, or maybe it was all in my head. I could only hope I never got so old that I wouldn't feel this uplifted.

By the time I found a parking spot several blocks from the jewelry store, I was belting my heart out to the Christmas songs on the radio. There was nobody around to roll their eyes and remind me I wasn't exactly the world's best singer. One tip for staying humble. Have children.

There were still a handful of shoppers in the store when I arrived, and I was the only woman, something that made me grin to myself—men looking for last-minute gifts for their wives and girlfriends. The clerk behind the counter opened the box holding Barrett's watch so I could take a look at the engraving on the back. *To Barrett, with all my love.*

"It's perfect," I murmured, admiring the delicate script. Sienna's earrings were beautiful, too, the sapphires sparkling richly in contrast to the creamy pearls. I hoped she would want to wear them. If not now, maybe one day when she was a little older and could appreciate them more.

It was a relief to step outside and get away from all that testosterone. The sky was a brilliant blue, and the sun sparkled off the snow that dusted the massive, decorated tree in the center of the village. Across from it, ice skaters guided along effortlessly while cheerful holiday tunes played from speakers set up at the rink's corners.

Only one thing could dampen my spirits on a day like this. The sudden, unwelcome addition of a voice that wasn't exactly familiar to me but was recognizable just the same. "Oh, hi there," Kelvin called out as he approached from the next store down from where I stood. Dammit. I should've gone straight for the car.

Do not engage. Do not let him get to you. That was so much easier said than done when the sight of his knowing smile turned my stomach. If he wasn't careful, he would end up with my lunch all over his loafers. "Small world," I offered with a brief, tight smile. The one I reserved for people I would rather never see again. It occurred to me that I should ask for my scarf, but then I didn't want to give him an excuse to spend more time together at his car if he even had it with him.

"It sure seems to be," he agreed. "I hope you're enjoying your Christmas Eve. You seem to be," he added, glancing at the shopping bag hanging from my hand.

"Last-minute shopping, you know how it is. How about you?" I asked. "Picking up gifts for your wife?"

His brow knitted together for a second, just long enough for me to know I knocked him off his game. "Among other things, yes," he replied once he recovered.

"Otherwise," I continued, "I might think you were following me around the village, and that would be strange."

Let him deny it. I hoped he would. Nothing would've been sweeter than to watch him sputter and struggle for an explanation that wouldn't make him look like the prime piece of shit he was.

The thing was, he didn't seem to care what a piece of shit he looked like. I knew that when he practically pinned me to the store window, meaning

I would have to squeeze past him if I wanted to get away, which I did, most definitely. "Would you be offended if I said I was?" he asked in a low, intimate tone that turned my stomach.

"Offended? No," I decided, lifting my chin. "Maybe a little concerned for you. Sorry for you, too," I added. "Because you're wasting your time."

His eyes crawled over my face as he replied, "I don't see it that way."

"With all due respect, Kelvin, I don't remember asking how you see it. I am telling you how it is. I don't know why you've taken this interest in me, but it needs to stop." My voice was shaking, but it wasn't out of fear. I could've happily clawed his eyes out.

"Is it so wrong, wanting to build a relationship with you since we'll be working together?" he asked with a smirk.

"Strange. I didn't know that had been confirmed yet."

"It hasn't been, but it will be soon. Let's stop kidding ourselves," he said with a laugh that made his breath form a cloud of fog between us. "We both know you're going to get it. Even if Alex wasn't familiar with your work, he loves the optics. Husband and wife both involved in the same project."

His gaze softened with that skin-crawling intimacy that left my stomach churning again. "It would be so much more fun working together if we could get a little closer, get to know each other. Wouldn't it?"

"I don't think so." I moved to the left, planning on making my escape, but the sudden appearance of his arm barred my way. He pressed his hand to the glass, leaning in, while I had to wonder why the hell nobody noticed what was going on. Screaming would start more problems than it was worth.

"Let me buy a cup of coffee, at least," he urged. "We could talk about your plans for the hotel."

"No. Now get out of my way." I was so close to losing it, shaking, biting my tongue against all the many things I wanted to say. I had to think of Olivia. I didn't want to lose this opportunity for her.

"He keeps you on that short of a leash, huh?"

There were a lot of things I was willing to put up with. This wasn't one of them. "I know you did not bring my husband into this," I whispered as my shaking intensified. "Wait, what am I saying? I know you did because I know you tried to start something a couple of days ago. You can keep the scarf because it's as much of me as you are ever going to get. You are vile, you are nasty, and you are wasting your time. Get out of my face."

He barely flinched at my insults, though he did scowl. "That's not going to do much for your chances at scoring a new project, you know."

"I don't care." God, it felt freeing to say that. "You can keep the goddamn hotel and decorate it yourself for all I care. If it means having to pretend to put up with your juvenile shit, I want nothing to do with it."

"I take it I can tell my brother-in-law you've withdrawn your name from consideration, then?"

"Kelvin, I don't care what you tell your brother-in-law," I replied with a smile. For once, it was genuine. "I have officially stopped giving a shit. Now you are going to move, and you are going to let me by without touching me, or I'm going to start screaming. It's up to you."

His gaze started over my face, but I was unflinching, staring straight back at him even though my heart raced and cold that had nothing to do with the temperature seeped into my bones. There was no going back. I had ruined it. I would have to find a way to make it up to Olivia.

"Have it your way." He pushed off the window, finally giving me room to walk past him. I moved on without a backward glance, relieved to have it over with but full of dread for what my best friend would say when I told her we wouldn't get the job after all. At least I'd be able to look my reflection in the eye every morning, knowing I hadn't compromised myself.

I could only hope that would be enough.

8

BARRETT

"I need somebody to keep watch for me." For the first time all evening, Lourde seemed genuinely excited as she raced up the stairs. The older boys were out, having parted ways with us after dinner, and the girls were in their rooms for the night. They had been warned not to peek at their gifts before tomorrow morning, something they rolled their eyes at but were smart enough not to gripe about, at least not in front of their mothers.

"Don't worry," I told her. "If I see anyone coming, I'll warn you." She was like a kid herself, something which eased my concerns after she'd spent our delicious Christmas Eve feast withdrawn, distracted. It was a dinner I knew she had looked forward to for weeks, maybe months, ever since we decided to come out here for the holiday. The village tree had glowed beyond the restaurant windows. The food was delicious, and there was an infectious energy in the air. Even the skaters and carolers hadn't been enough to stir a smile that lasted more than a second or two.

She and Ari crossed paths on the stairs, and he chuckled as she dashed past him, but by the time he met my gaze, his expression hardened. He discreetly jerked his chin toward the door, heading straight in that direction while I followed. *Now what?*

"Somebody else keep an eye out for me for a minute," I told the rest of the room with a wink and a chuckle, stepping out into the cold, clear night. The sky was full of stars and a ripe, full moon that painted the world silver.

Ari looked unimpressed. "We have a problem." He glanced toward the window like he was making sure no one was watching or listening. "I just got a call from the police station. It seems our sons decided to tear it up in the village and wound up in a fight outside a pub."

On fucking Christmas Eve, of all nights while their mothers raced around to gather their presents for under the tree. "Were they arrested?" I gritted out.

"Yes, they were. They're currently waiting for us to bail them out. Merry Christmas," he deadpanned.

One thing was obvious—Lourde couldn't know about this. "I'm guessing you're not telling Olivia?" I muttered.

"Please. She would already be halfway there by now, ready to take him over her knee in front of everybody at the station." He ran a hand over his jaw, then sighed. "To tell you the truth, at the moment, I wouldn't blame her. I would like to take a turn, myself."

"What the fuck was he thinking?" I asked myself, though I knew it was a stupid question. My son loved behaving the way my son behaved—recklessly, with no thought for how his actions would affect the people who cared about him. Like his mother, placing gifts around the tree for him. This would break her heart, and she already seemed distracted and a little sad. "We'll have to wait until the women go to sleep," I decided. "I don't think it will kill the kids to spend a little time thinking about what they did."

"When I get Noah in front of me, I swear." Ari's jaw tightened, and his eyes narrowed. "He wants to be a big man, strut around, start fights in pubs? Then he's going to be treated like a man."

That was fine and good, but at the moment, we had to play this off for the sake of our wives. The distraction of arranging gifts around the tree was a welcome one. Once Ari shared the news with the other men, the four of us could do nothing but exchange tense looks while pretending everything was fine.

I would make Colton wish he had never stepped foot out of this cabin tonight. Who the hell did he think he was? Did he ever think at all?

"What's wrong?" Now, it was Lourde asking me the same question I asked her more than once earlier that night. She came to me and draped her arms around my waist once she was satisfied with the stack of gifts she had arranged. "Don't worry. There are plenty of tags with your name on them," she teased.

"You should know by now I don't need gifts. I already have everything." I kissed the top of her head, glancing toward the antique clock hanging above the hearth. It was coming up on one in the morning. The boys had been waiting a couple of hours. I didn't know how much longer I could keep up the act.

Pepper threw her arms overhead, stretching as

she got up from the floor. "That's it for me. I'm beat. See you all in the morning."

Olivia looked like she was going to follow Pepper's and Connor's lead, but she frowned when Ari didn't join her. "I think I might stay up for a little while longer," he explained. There wasn't a hint of the strain he was in when he kissed her forehead. "I'll be up soon."

"Same here," I decided. The women exchanged curious looks.

"Okay, but no matter what surprise you have up your sleeves..." Lourde giggled, starting up the stairs, "... don't be too long," she warned, winking before jogging the rest of the way.

Then it was Ari and me in front of the twinkling tree surrounded by gifts, about to do something neither of us looked forward to. It was a fairly simple process—show up at the police station, explain who we were, and come to an understanding with the chief. "This isn't the kind of thing they normally do," I explained while we waited for the boys to join us. "I know you probably hear that a lot, but in this case, it's the truth."

"They ran into a bunch of their friends from school out here," Ari explained. "They wanted to impress them, I'm guessing."

"Yeah, well, the fistfight that broke out in front of the pub wasn't so impressive." Chief Perkins scratched the top of his head, sighing. "But there was no property damage. The other guy's going to have a black eye in the morning, and your son has a busted lip, but nobody's pressing charges," he told me.

"What were they thinking?" Ari shook his head, muttering under his breath.

I had a pretty damn good idea, considering my son was the only one injured. It certainly had me seething by the time the door leading farther back into the station swung open. A tall, uniformed officer walked through, followed by three shame-faced young men. Colton barely glanced my way before looking back down at the floor. Sure enough, somebody had popped him in the mouth, and I had a feeling it was not an unprovoked attack.

I wanted nothing more than to embarrass the shit out of him in front of everyone in earshot, but I didn't need rumors flying around about Barrett Black being an abusive prick of a father, either. Instead, the five of us left the station and didn't say a word until we were outside.

"Let me guess what happened," I offered as we rounded the station on the way to the parking lot. "One of you said the wrong thing to someone else.

You were a little drunk, underage," I added with a growl. "Someone looked at you the wrong way or said the wrong thing, and you invited him to take it outside so you could settle it like men. Is that more or less the story?"

The way Noah and Evan stared at the ground told me it was, indeed, the story. "He was a dick," Colton spat.

"Bryce Harper. He's the older brother of one of our friends from home," Noah explained. "He called us out for getting in underage and shoved us outside. He shoved Colton the hardest, and that's when Colton took a swing."

"He was putting you in your place," I told my son, who had the nerve to roll his eyes.

"I don't need anybody putting in my place," he muttered.

"I wouldn't be so sure about that." We looked at each other before I slid behind the wheel, and he climbed into the back seat. Ari hadn't said much of anything, too busy shaking his head and muttering as he took the passenger seat.

"Sorry, Mr. Black," Evan offered from the back, between Colton and Noah.

"I'm sure you are," I replied as I turned out of the parking lot and headed back to the cabin. "You're also lucky we were able to get things settled. Do any of you understand what happens to people who get drunk and start fights in bars? Do you want to throw away your entire future in some stupid, avoidable accident? Do you think any of you will remember this come next Christmas?"

"Next Christmas?" Ari snickered. "They won't remember by the Fourth of July."

"Sometimes, you have to be the bigger man," I concluded. "Yea, there are going to be times in your life when you want more than anything to kick the shit out of somebody." No big surprise who came to mind when I said that. That smug smile Kelvin gave me at the lodge, daring me to do something about him spending time with my wife.

"Being a man means ignoring that impulse," Ari concluded while his hands tightened into fists in his lap. "Sucker punch a man who's had too much to drink, and he can go down like a sack of bricks and crack his head open. That could've gone much worse than it did. I hope, sincerely, that this is a lesson for all of you."

We passed the rest of the short ride in tense silence after that, with at least two of us imagining how much uglier the whole situation might have turned out.

The idea was to sneak the boys back into the cabin without the women being the wiser, but then I hadn't counted on Olivia pouring herself a drink by the fireplace when we arrived. She was in her pajamas and bathrobe, telling me she had at least gone through the motions of getting ready for bed.

"What's going on?" Ari asked, going to her once he was out of his coat.

Olivia ran a distracted hand through her hair, groaning. "I just got a terrific Christmas present." Her fair cheeks were flushed, though something told me it had nothing to do with the alcohol. Her snarl spoke volumes. Noah gulped behind me, and Evan made a choked sound.

Ari ran a hand over the back of Olivia's head while the rest of us watched silently, waiting for the inevitable explosion. How had she found out? "Sweetheart, everything will be fine. We–"

"I know it will be fine," she snapped. "That doesn't mean I have to like being thrown out of competition for the Schwartz project."

"Wait, what?" I asked.

"Dammit. She didn't want you to find out this way." She took a gulp of her drink, then set the glass down with a sigh. "Lourde told me after you left.

Kelvin Barnes practically stalked her today, cornered her in the village, and propositioned her."

"Shit," Colton whispered.

I could agree. "What else happened?" I asked. The anger already simmering in my chest turned to rage that threatened to blind me. "What did he do?"

"Nothing but making disgusting comments," she spat. "So she told him to shove the job up his ass if he thought she would sleep with him to get it."

"Boys, upstairs," Ari ordered, herding them like cattle and moving them to the stairs. "In the morning, none of this happened. Go."

"She probably didn't want to bring it up until after tomorrow," Olivia mused as the boys shuffled up the stairs. "I wish she had said something earlier. I would kick that guy in the balls hard enough to lodge them in his fucking throat."

She'd have to wait in line. I wanted the first crack at him.

"He was dangling the job in front of her, that bastard." She must have taken my murderous expression the wrong way since she looked stricken when she touched my arm. "Don't be mad at her. None of this is her fault."

"I'm not mad at her." A drink wasn't a bad idea. I

poured one for myself with a shaking hand. "I'm going to kill him."

"So long as I can watch." The anger seemed to drain from her all at once, and now disappointment took its place. "Dammit. That fucker."

"Come here." Ari wrapped her in a hug, resting his chin on the top of her head and exchanging a look with me. "There will be plenty of opportunities for you two. I know how much you wanted it, but it's not the end all, be all."

"I know." She tapped the side of her fist against his chest. "It's just so damn unfair. I know we could kill it, but we can't because some asshole decided to use the situation to get his dick wet. What a pig. I just can't stand the idea of him winning."

"He hasn't won shit," I decided, gulping back half of my scotch. What a fucking night this was turning into. I wasn't exactly in a *Peace on Earth, Good Will Toward Men* mood.

"He's probably robbed us of the opportunity to decorate that hotel," she reminded me. "What would you call it?"

"It doesn't matter. He's going to regret the day he decided to fuck with Lourde," I vowed, draining my glass. The burn of the scotch was nothing compared to the burning coal lodged in my chest.

"Remember, Dad." I hadn't noticed Colton lingering at the top of the stairs rather than going to his room. His smirk told me exactly what he was going to say before he opened his mouth. "Whatever happened to being the bigger man?"

"Do yourself a favor and get to bed," I warned. "And if you happen to see your mother, don't say a word about any of this." If anything, he looked glad to be dismissed without any more berating from me. With him back at the cabin, safe, he was officially the least of my worries.

"What are you going to do?" Ari asked when I pulled my phone from my pocket. Olivia chewed her lip, watching intently.

"I'm not sure," I admitted. It was past one in the morning, after all, and there was no telling I'd be successful. But I had to try.

By the time I was finished with him, Kelvin Barnes would wish he was never born.

9

———

LOURDE

"Oh, Lourde." There was soft wonder in Barrett's voice as he took the watch from its box and examined it, a soft smile playing over his lips, his eyes shining. "It's gorgeous. How did you know I've been wanting a Patek Philippe?"

I waved a hand, laughing softly. "You mentioned it months ago, and I made a note in my phone. Do you like it?"

"I love it." He put it on and held out his arm, grinning as he admired it. "It's gorgeous. It was thoughtful of you to remember. But then I shouldn't be surprised." He kissed the tip of my nose, enfolding me in a hug. "Thank you."

If my heart got any fuller, it would explode. Right

now, it looked like the only explosion that had taken place so far occurred in the living room. Noah admired his new ski equipment, Colton was setting up his new gaming laptop, and the twins were ecstatic with their clothes and purses. Evan looked a little overwhelmed. His parents had shipped his gifts out here before they left for their European trip, and we had supplemented that with a few things Colton suggested he might like. The kids had also bought gifts for each other, and of course, there were the gifts exchanged by the adults.

There was a special sort of chaos taking place all around us.

"Mom. These are really beautiful." Sienna was holding the box containing her new earrings. "They're just like the ones you have at home."

"I was hoping you would notice. That's why I bought them, so we could almost match." She didn't shrink back when I wrapped my arms around her and gave her a tight hug. "Merry Christmas, sweetheart. Are you happy with your gifts?"

Her head bobbed, and she looked genuinely happy for the first time all week. "Everything is awesome." She kissed my cheek, making my entire holiday. I didn't need another thing. I had it all.

My husband had other ideas.

"I have one last gift for you, Dollface." He took my face in his hands, and something in his eyes took my breath away. The depth of love I saw. Sometimes, it was almost too much for my heart to handle.

"You practically bought me a new wardrobe," I pointed out. "And boots, and purses, and a weekend spa package. You don't think you've already given me enough?" I looked around at all the crumpled wrapping paper, ribbons, and bows. Joyous laughter filled the air like music. My children were happy. Our friends were beaming. What else could I possibly need?

"Not quite yet, no." He shook his head. "There's one more thing I can't wait to give you."

Something about his choice of words made me lift an eyebrow. "You've been giving me that gift for a long time now," I reminded him in a whisper.

"I don't mean that, though I was hoping we could have a little Christmas night fun later." He winked, then nodded toward the stairs. "But I do want you to go up there and get dressed. I'll have to take you to your gift."

This was getting more confusing and interesting by the second. "All right, let me put some clothes on." I dashed up the stairs, filled with anticipation. As it turned out, it was possible for a woman in her early forties to feel as excited as a kid on Christmas morning.

After throwing on some clothes and grabbing a croissant from the pastry tray we'd ordered especially for this morning, I headed out with Barrett in the lead. Everybody seemed as confused and amused as I was, everybody but Olivia, who had been strangely cagey. She was having a great morning, but every time our eyes met, she looked away. Had I ruined things by telling her about Kelvin? Was she upset with me?

Another question bubbled up in my head, and now that we were away from everyone else, I asked my husband, "Tell me again what happened to Colton's lip? It looks like he got in a fight."

He shrugged, opening the passenger door so I could get in. "Something about an argument with a friend's brother. Kid stuff." I was willing to believe that, though it would've been nice to get a family photo that didn't include a busted lip. One day, when he had kids of his own, he would understand.

The drive took only five minutes when a familiar hotel materialized on the horizon. We weren't going *there,* were we? Sure enough, we came closer, finally turning into the driveway leading up to the main building. "I don't get it," I admitted. Staring up at the hotel as we approached, I was filled with more questions than ever. "What is this all about? Is my gift here?"

It was infuriating the way he refused to answer until we were parked in front of the entrance. "Listen to me for a second." He put the SUV in park and killed the engine, then angled his body in his seat until he was facing me. "I know what happened."

My lungs emptied all at once, and soon, I could only fall back against my seat with an unhappy sigh. "I didn't want you to find out that way. I was going to tell you. I didn't want to ruin—"

He only shook his head and touched a finger to his lips. "Nothing is ruined. I'm sorry you had to hold all of that inside. I wish you would've told me. We could've talked it out and salvaged your night."

"The night was fine." Though I could've been more present, telling Barrett the whole ugly story wouldn't have changed anything. I would still have been angry and resentful.

I looked out through the windshield, still as confused as ever. The towering, silent hotel wasn't offering any answers. "All right, so why are we actually here? Don't tell me you have Kelvin tied up inside, ready to be tortured." The idea didn't upset me.

"Wait and see." He opened his door and hopped out, jogging around to my side and opening my door. "All will be revealed inside." I was beyond confused but also intrigued as we walked hand in hand into the lobby. The door was unlocked, something that didn't surprise me. Not much would surprise me today. I decided to stop trying to guess and just go with it.

"Good morning. Merry Christmas." Alex Schwartz emerged from an office behind the front desk, a steaming mug in hand. He was wearing one of the gaudiest sweaters I'd ever seen, complete with Rudolph and his blinking nose. "How has the holiday treated you so far?"

"Just fine. Thank you for agreeing to meet up here this morning." Barrett shook his hand while I looked on, mute with confusion. "Did everything look okay to you?" he asked.

Alex nodded firmly. "Beyond generous."

Barrett beamed. "Excellent. Once the team is back in the office after the holidays, we can firm up the finer points."

"Exactly what is going on?" I asked as the front door swung open, bringing with it a burst of cold air and Kelvin Barnes.

My heart went still for a second. I forgot how to

breathe, grabbing Barrett's hand to hold him in place. I wasn't sure why I bothered. It wasn't like I would be able to keep him still if he decided to take a swing at Kelvin for what he did. The last thing we needed was a fight, especially on Christmas morning.

"Oh. Good morning. I didn't expect anyone else to be here besides my brother-in-law." Kelvin shot Alex a puzzled look as he unwound his scarf. "What's going on? You said it was important."

"It is important," Alex told him. Like magic, his jovial attitude dissolved. "I want you to tell me the truth. Have you been offering jobs you are in no position to offer?"

"What?" Kelvin laughed. "I'm not sure what you're talking about. Who would I offer a job to?"

"My wife and her business partner, for starters," Barrett replied. There was anger in his voice, yes, but it wasn't nearly what I would've expected after what Kelvin did. Hell, he'd sounded angrier with me in our bedroom when confronting me. "Are you going to stand here and pretend you didn't tell her you would get her the job because you... how did you put it? Looked forward to working together? Did you or did you not proposition her yesterday?"

"Why would I do that? I'm a happily married

man!" Kelvin even touched a hand to his chest like he was genuinely stunned, glaring at me. "What, do you think you're going to get this job by lying your way into it? Accusing me? There I was, thinking your work stood for itself."

He was truly despicable, lying to my face and pretending we didn't both know the truth. I was too overwhelmed by hatred to say a word.

"It's all right," Barrett told me, squeezing my hand while wearing a Mona Lisa smile. "That's all over now. Merry Christmas."

Just when I thought I couldn't be more baffled. "I don't understand."

"You and Olivia will decorate this hotel," he explained. "Because it's our hotel now."

It took a second. More than a second. I had to be imagining things or mishearing him, something. Maybe I was still in bed. Maybe we hadn't gone downstairs to open presents yet, and this was all a dream.

Kelvin barked out a disbelieving laugh. "Oh, come on. You can't be serious."

"He is," Alex explained. "I sold Barrett the hotel. He made me an offer overnight."

The man's face went white as a sheet. "But... you

would never sell! After everything you went through to get the funding together and—"

"As it turns out, there's a price for everything," Barrett told him. "What I offered for the sale of this hotel will be more than enough for Alex here to buy an entire chain if he feels like it. And he'll still run day-to-day operations, but *without* you," he concluded, his voice almost acidic. "Lourde and I will handle all such decisions about staffing, and you've already proven you can't be trusted."

"I won't tell your sister about this," Alex added with disdain dripping from his voice, "For her sake, not yours. Your wife doesn't need to know, either, since nothing came of this but you making an ass of yourself. As for why you are no longer working with me in any capacity, I'll let you make up a reason on your own, but again, if you decide to make me the bad guy and turn her against me, she'll learn everything. Got it?"

"Sorry to ruin your holiday," Barrett concluded with a smile. "What am I saying? I'm not sorry at all. I'm rarely sorry for people who bring things like this upon themselves."

Holy shit. He bought me a hotel.

I was swaying on my feet, totally dazed. I wouldn't have imagined this in a hundred years. Just like I couldn't have imagined the deep satisfaction of watching Kelvin Barnes slink away once he knew he was beat. As much as I would've liked to be the one to put him in his place, it was enough to witness it happening.

Barrett turned to me, searching for my reaction, when all I could do was stare blankly at the door Kelvin had walked through. "Are you happy?" he asked.

Was I? "Yes," I decided. "But... I mean, isn't this sort of cheating? I wanted to get the job on my own. Not because my husband bought the place."

"If it makes you feel better," Alex offered. "I had already decided to use you and Olivia, and not because of anything Kelvin said. To tell you the truth, we never discussed it. I wouldn't have taken his thoughts into consideration. He's useless. I only kept him around to make my wife happy."

"That's very nice of you to say." But I still wasn't convinced.

"Here. Maybe this will help." He pulled out his phone and tapped the screen a few times, then held it out to me. "See? This email is from four days ago. I told my business manager back in New York that I had decided to go with you two for this."

He wasn't lying. Our names were right there on

an email dated the twenty-first. "Oh. Wow. Thank you," I breathed out. It sounded awkward and a little empty, but it was all I could come up with. "Thank you so much for your faith in us."

"And now," Barrett concluded with a smile. "You know it would've been yours if it hadn't been for a certain someone standing in your way."

I thanked Alex again, still a little dazed by the time we left. I managed to wait until we were in the vehicle before turning to my husband. "You know, you could've just gotten him fired," I pointed out. "You didn't have to go that far, buying an entire hotel."

"You're right," he admitted with a shrug and a roguish grin that made his eyes sparkle. "But then *I* wouldn't have been able to fire him. That was what I wanted most. And I wanted you there while it happened. Plus, Alex gets to expand even further now. This is a win all the way around."

"Well, it was nice to watch him lose," I admitted.

"As for buying the entire hotel…" He reached out, his hands on my shoulders so he could turn me to face him. There was that look in his eye again. All that love. "Don't you know there's no limit to what I would do for you? I'd buy you a chain of hotels. An entire city's worth if that was what you wanted. I know this project meant a lot to you. I know how much you want to expand your business, and I want that for you. But I would not, under any circumstances, put up with you being treated like a piece of meat or a pawn in some game. A way to get back at me. When it comes to you, I will stop at nothing. You don't know that by now?"

I did know it. Sometimes, it still took me by surprise. "I guess we own a hotel now."

"I guess we do. And I guess you and Olivia are going to be *very* busy." He started the engine and backed out of the parking space. "She doesn't know about any of this, only that I was calling Alex when she went to bed. Why don't you tell her when we get back to the cabin?" he suggested.

I could hardly wait.

10

BARRETT

"Are you happy tonight?" I pulled my wife a little closer to me, my hand against the bare skin of her back, thanks to the way the dress plunged almost all the way down to the base of her spine. It was hardly the most revealing thing I had seen since the New Year's Eve Ball started, which only made it sexier. It revealed plenty but left plenty more to the imagination.

Not to my imagination, of course. I had already cataloged every square inch of the woman's body and was always ready to re-explore.

"Ecstatic," she said, wearing a dreamy sort of smile when she tipped her head back to look up at me. Her graceful neck was on display thanks to her upswept hair, and the diamond necklace I'd gifted her for Christmas gleamed against her creamy skin.

"Good. The perfect way to go into the new year." I drew her close again, and we continued to dance to the slow, romantic standard played by the band. The room was fully decked out with countless trees, garland, and bows. Twinkling lights were strung across the ceiling from one end of the ballroom to the other, adding to the ambiance already created by hundreds of candles.

Everyone was here, dancing and mingling, digesting the lavish meals we had enjoyed. The kids had enjoyed dancing during the last string of upbeat songs but now hung around the edges of the floor, all dressed in their black-tie finest. I couldn't believe how mature they looked.

"I think we all needed this," I mused, spotting Connor and Pepper, Evelyn and Magnus. Ari and Olivia danced past us and Olivia winked at Lourde when Ari twirled her away. "We need to step away from life and reset. All of us."

"That's so true. And we've made great memories," Lourde pointed out with a happy sigh. Including another skiing race, this time involving the women as well as the men. We had gone skating, built a snowman in front of the cabin, which had turned into a snowball fight in the end, and basically acted like kids the entire week between Christmas and New Year's.

"Just think. You're starting off the new year with a great new project, and the possibilities are endless after that." I squeezed her, filled with immeasurable love. I could try for the rest of my life and never find the words to truly capture how she made me feel. "Do you know how proud I am of you? I'm serious. How proud I am every single day?"

"You're pretty good at showing me," she confessed. "You never leave me wondering how you feel."

"Good. Because I want to make sure that every day, all your life, you know exactly how incredible you are. Brilliant, creative, loving."

Taking a deep breath, I savored her sweet, slightly spicy perfume. "And, if you don't mind my saying, the hottest woman alive."

"For the record?" There was a light in her eyes that matched the playful smile stretching her crimson-painted lips. "I'll never mind hearing that, even if I don't quite believe you."

"What do I have to do to convince you?" I asked.

"Maybe I should ravish you here and now, on the dance floor in front of all these people."

"All right, that would be officially taking things too far." She giggled.

"Then how about we go someplace private?" Leaning down, I whispered in her ear, "Because if I am not inside you by the time the clock strikes midnight, I might die from the most extreme case of blue balls in history."

Her cheeks flushed. "Dump a couple glasses of champagne down your throat, and you turn into a very dramatic person, Mr. Black."

Considering she took my hand and led me back to our table to grab her purse, I had the feeling she didn't mind my flare for the dramatic. With an excuse about a headache, she wished Colton and Sienna a happy new year once we found them around the dance floor perimeter. "And I want you straight back to the cabin with the rest of the adults," she added, shooting Colton a hard look. "No stragglers."

"Are you sure you want to do this?" I asked, even as we hurried our way out of the ballroom. "You don't want to stick around for midnight?"

"After what you described to me?" she asked with a laugh. "We have a medical emergency on our hands. And there's still another half hour to go, so who knows how much worse it would get by the time midnight comes around?"

Who was I to argue?

One of the drivers we'd hired for the evening took us to the cabin before heading back to the ball to wait for the others, leaving us entirely on our own. After the past eleven days of nonstop noise, the silence greeting us when we entered was almost eerie.

I didn't take any time to ponder over it. There were more important things to do. I had barely closed the door when my hands were on her, touching her the way I had longed to do ever since she descended the stairs wearing the curve-hugging black gown, which I now could not wait to get off her.

"Not here," she whispered between hot, urgent kisses, sliding my tuxedo jacket off my shoulders as we traveled across the room and toward the stairs. "I don't need the kids coming back and seeing my dress in a puddle on the floor."

"Then you better get that fine ass of yours upstairs, *now*." When I lunged, she flew up the stairs, laughing while I followed.

She was already reaching behind her to unfasten

the thick straps that met at the back of her neck by the time I reached the bedroom. That was all it took for the entire garment to fall to her ankles, leaving her in nothing but a black lace thong. She was silhouetted perfectly in the light of a half-moon hanging over her shoulder beyond the window.

"You are the most beautiful thing I've ever seen," I told her, my eyes moving over her body while I tossed my bow aside and then unfastened the new cufflinks the kids had given me for Christmas. My dick was throbbing, begging for relief as I watched her crawl onto the king-size bed from the opposite side of where I stood, then she seductively made her way to me on her hands and knees.

"I believe you said something about blue balls?" she whispered, eyeing the erection now tenting my pants as I removed my shirt. Her teeth sank into her bottom lip, and I growled in response, my blood humming, my cock throbbing with every beat of my heart.

"Take a look and see for yourself," I invited, making her settle on her knees so she could use her hands to open my pants and let them drop, followed by my boxer briefs. Clicking her tongue, she said, "It's a good thing we didn't wait any longer. This is a serious case."

Then she took me in her mouth, treating me to a few long, slow strokes while her tongue worked magic on the underside of my shaft. "Fuck..." I groaned, closing my eyes, letting her work me like only she could. On her hands and knees, her back arched so her ass lifted into the air. I sank my hands into her hair, removing the clip holding it in place so the waves could tumble down. "That's right. Suck my cock. You make me feel so fucking good." Lustful moans vibrated through me.

It would have been easy to let her go, to lose myself to her mouth and the low. But there was so much more I wanted to do, so many ways I wanted to hear her say my name, which was why I lifted her away from me with a growl. "Turn around. Hands and knees. I need to see if your pussy is ready for me."

"Oh, it is," she purred, slowly turning around the way she was told until her magnificent ass was in front of me. Her soft, needful sighs filled the air while I ran my hands over those smooth, firm globes. She was always so ready to feel good like her entire body was primed for pleasure. For me. The slightest brush of my fingers against the curve of her ass or the backs of her thighs left her helplessly moaning before I pulled the thong down to her knees.

Fuck she was wet. Her bald lips glistened in the moonlight, evidence of her need for me. Her readiness for me. But first, I sank to my knees like a man about to pray. Or worship.

"Oh, sh-it!" she cried out, pushing back against my face when I probed her slit with my tongue. "Eat me," she begged, moaning louder when my fingers pressed hard against her ass cheeks.

There was so much to play with. So much fun to be had. I moved over her body with my hands while my tongue worked her pussy. I cupped her tits, scraped my nails down her back, and spread her cheeks wider so I could drive my tongue deep inside her quivering sheath. Every time she moaned my name, it made me want to give her more. All she could take.

"Just like that," she pleaded in a frantic whisper, grinding faster, almost sloppy, once she reached the point of no return. When instinct took over for everything else, driving her body and soul toward one goal. Release.

And when she reached it, she howled, swinging her head so her hair tumbled like a waterfall across her back. "Yes!" She whined as a rush of sweet nectar coated my tongue. I was greedy for it, licking up everything I could reach, filling my senses with her while she whimpered in the aftermath—one that didn't last long.

She was still coming down when I entered her, driving myself deep. "Still coming for me?" I whispered, taking her by the hips and pulling her back hard enough to make her yelp. "You going to come on my cock?"

"Yes..." She moaned, writhing, moonlight dancing off her skin.

Fuck, this was all I wanted every day for the rest of my life. Being inside her, feeling her grip me tight, drawing me deeper. The sense of being exactly where I belonged, united with this perfect woman— it never got old.

Before she could come, I pulled out and rolled her onto her back. I needed to hold her. To kiss and caress, to stare into her eyes and watch as she lost herself to me. She cradled my body with hers, wrapping her legs around me and pulling in, silently begging for more.

This was better. Teasing her mouth with my tongue, I took her with short, shallow strokes that left her whining with need. "Fuck me," she begged, her voice a throaty whisper. "Fuck me hard. Give me your cock."

"Don't be in such a hurry," I whispered, dragging the tip of my tongue across the seam of her mouth until she whimpered in frustration. She moved beneath me, nails dragging across my shoulders and down my back.

"I want to come... make me come..." Her hips jerked upward, trying to draw me deeper, to find her release. But not yet.

Not until I was ready.

It was only when the first burst of shimmering color and light filled the sky that I pushed up onto my forearms and drove myself deep and hard. "Happy New Year," I grunted out while another colorful explosion lit the sky, then another. Gold, silver, red—the colors flashed across the room and our bodies while I took her in hard, almost punishing strokes that soon had us both moaning, panting, working together to reach the end.

And when we did, she clutched me tight, crying out helplessly, her pussy milking me dry. I let go gladly, pouring myself into her until we were both almost limp, breathless.

"Happy New Year," she whispered while the fireworks continued.

We turned our heads to watch, wrapped in each other, wrapped in love and the promise of the new year to come...

... and every year after that.

THE END.

ALSO BY MISSY WALKER

ELITE HEIRS OF MANHATTAN SERIES

Seductive Hearts

Sweet Surrender

Sinful Desires

Silent Cravings

Sensual Games

Endless Love

ELITE MEN OF MANHATTAN SERIES

Forbidden Lust*

Forbidden Love*

Lost Love

Missing Love

Guarded Love

Infinite Love Novella

A White Christmas

ELITE MAFIA OF NEW YORK SERIES

Cruel Lust*

Stolen Love

Finding Love

SLATER SIBLINGS SERIES

Hungry Heart

Chained Heart

Iron Heart

SMALL TOWN DESIRES SERIES

Trusting the Rockstar

Trusting the Ex

Trusting the Player

*Forbidden Lust/Love are a duet and to be read in order.

*Cruel Lust is a trilogy and to be read in order

All other books are stand alones.

JOIN MISSY'S BOOK BABES

Hear about exclusive book releases, teasers, discounts and book bundles before anyone else.

Sign up to Missy's newsletter here:
www.authormissywalker.com

Become part of Missy's Facebook Reader Group where we chat all things books, releases and of course fun giveaways!

https://www.facebook.com/groups/
missywalkersbookbabes

ACKNOWLEDGMENTS

This was my first Christmas book and it was so fun to delve back into the world of Lourde and Barrett. They may be older, but still so hot for one another:)

A huge thanks to my editors, Chantell, Kay, and Nicki, for your feedback. I love how you push me with every.single.book!

To my amazing betas, Ella, Karmin, Maria, and Saskia, for your comments and unwavering commitment to my ridiculous deadlines.

To my fans, especially my Facebook reader group, Missy Walker's Book Babes—building this community has been incredible, and I love everything you share.

Much love,
Missy x

ABOUT THE AUTHOR

Missy is an Australian author who writes kissing books with equal parts angst and steam. Stories about billionaires, forbidden romance, and second chances roll around in her mind probably more than they ought to.

When she's not writing, she's taking care of her two daughters and doting husband and conjuring up her next saucy plot.

Inspired by the acreage she lives on, Missy regularly distracts herself by visiting her orchard, baking naughty but delicious foods, and socialising with her girl squad.

Then there's her overweight cat—Charlie, chickens, and border collie dog—Benji if she needed another excuse to pass the time.

If you like Missy Walker's books, consider leaving a review and following her here:

instagram.com/missywalkerauthor
facebook.com/AuthorMissyWalker
tiktok.com/@authormissywalker
bookbub.com/profile/missy-walker